Set in the USA, this story is of an American girl Kim from a middle-class family, who because of the attitude of the people around her is made to believe that her parents are going to get divorced. It's about 4th graders, who at their innocent age play pranks on their teachers. The way they try to act older than their age.

In this book, the gals are tomboys and the guys are the baby kind. There is a romantic angle too, one of the girls falls in love with her teacher, and gets jealous of one of the lady teachers. There are lots of episodes where the girls are braver than the guys.

A must for all youngsters who love to read, especially for girls. Tomboys for sure will love it. A light piece, full of jocular school incidents, including field-trips, making fun of teachers and the Principal (which all school kids love to do), and lots and lots of other things.

Kiran Pallod is 19 years old, doing her Bachelors in Mass Communication from St. Francis, Hyderabad. She was 17 when she wrote this novel. She did her schooling from St. Ann's, Secunderabad. Kiran comes from a very loving joint family. She loves reading, watching English movies, listening to great music, dancing, playing basketball and lawn tennis.

Girls Go Wild

KIRAN PALLOD

PRESTIGE

PRESTIGE BOOKS
3/28, East Patel Nagar
New Delhi 110 008

ISBN: 81-7551-106-0

Printed at Chaman Offset Press, New Delhi 110 002

CONTENTS

for

my very dear family and friends

1

DINOSAUR DELIGHT

"You know what Dinosaur Delight sounds like? It sounds like ice cream with salted fossils." I told Nicky. "Just the *sound* hurts my teeth. I'd rather spend my Saturday cleaning the cat's box than going to a Dinosaur Delight."

Nicky Ryder was walking her front porch rail, tilting like a stunt airplane. She tipped, flapping her arms, and almost crashed into the junniper bushes. I was next door in my yard filling my bike tyres with fresh air after their long, flat summer. It has rained the night before, and worms lay on the sidewalk gagging for air.

"It was my *mother* who thought up that name!" Nicky yelled. She jumped to the porch and whipped a fat green rubber frog at me. It sailed way over my head. I couldn't have reached it with accordion arms. Goby, Nicky's little brother, ran after it into my yard.

"Frogger!" he shrieked. "Mine!" Goby is four and the frog *was* his.

"It's because my mom knew the fourth graders would be doing dinosaurs now," Nicky went on. "She said we'd go bananas over a fair called Dinosaur Delight. So that it just shows how much *you* know Kim Street."

"I know we studied almost an hour for the dumb test yesterday, and I know that's enough dinosaurs for me." I lifted the frog from Goby's clutch. "Besides, I'm going to ride my bike today all the way down the Greenland Trail."

Goby stamped on my foot. I dropped the frog on his head. Nicky and Goby's mother is big in the Central (Jail) school PTA. She's head of something called Ways and Means. That's a bunch of people, Nicky says, who figure out ways to make money. The Dinosaur Delight was one of those ways.

Actually, every winter the PTA throws a fair in the gym. Last year it was the Jungle Jumboree. My dad took me and wanted to leave after five minutes. The place was decorated with tons of crepe paper and pink-and-yellow snakes that curled down through the fans. My dad couldn't believe it. Pink-and-yellow snakes! People sold sandwiches and other stuff they'd made. But the worst part was a bunch of third and fourth grade boys dressed up like leopards who hopped around selling alligator whistles and chocolate in the form of animals. They made jungle type noises, held their hands up like paws, and thought they were incredibly cute. My dad said we should leave, before we stepped on one. "I won't go," I said pumping away on my back tyre. One more squirt of air, I thought, the tyre will be full and I'll be free. "Dinosaurs are extinct and I am glad."

Goby sat on the grass at my feet and ground dandelion heads on his knees, covering them with bright yellow dots. Then he reached over and twisted a splotch on the toe of my grungy gym shoe. "Hey, Kim, you know what?" he called up to me. "You like butter, too!"

"Kim Street!" Mom called out from the living room window. "Are you and your father going to the Dinosaur Delight thing with Nicky or not?"

"Come on," Nicky mumbled. "I'm not going to that by myself."

"No!" My dad called from the garden out back. "I've got a glitch in my side from too much digging."

"Great," she said. "Then you can help me take down the storm windows. I'll just send the money to school with Nicky."

"Do I have to?" I groaned.

Nicky grinned and jumped down the steps. "You can't mind, Street. When do we leave?"

"Oh, Kim, you know what else?" Mom said, sticking her head out again.

"Yeah, I know. I haven't changed Fido's litter."

"Right."

The early April sun was warm, but the air still smelled like it had just rained. Even on a good day, Fido's litter box does not smell like fresh rain. I had been pumping my back tyre for about five minutes, and it was still your basic flat back tyre. Something was wrong. If I'd pumped that much air into a kickball, it would have exploded.

"And your father needs some help in . . ." Mom started.

"I know. I know." Dinosaurs were beginning to sound like prime time T.V. Maybe the fair would be fabulous and not cutesie. Maybe none of the fourth grade boys would be wearing weird costumes and selling things.

"I've changed my mind," I told her, and she smiled. "I'll do all that stuff when I get back. Nicky would probably lose the money anyway."

Nicky flicked a black spider at me by the long rubber band in its back. Goby yanked out a handful of grass and started to sweep the sidewalk clear of worms.

Handing me a ten-dollar bill, Mom said that if they weren't gone I was to buy a dozen of Mrs. Fox's famous chewy walnut brownies that she made for every bake sale and to spend the rest the way I wanted to because it was for such a good cause. Then she went back to exchanging storm windows for screens.

After I'd stashed my sick bike in the garage, Nicky and I started out for school. It seemed weird on a Saturday morning. Especially at nine-thirty. We knew there wasn't gong to be a bell at the other end. Or a kickball game before the ball or Miss Planet with a spelling test.

"Hold up," Goby yelled. We turned and watched him scramble to his feet.

"You're not going with us," I called to him. "This is for the big kids." He stuck out his bottom up and sucked in through breath for a major shriek.

"Oh, didn't I tell you?" Nicky said, inspecting her gym shoes. "We're taking Goby." She went on fast. "Mom had to be there at seven thirty this morning to set up."

Goby can be a pain. He's got a whine like fingernails scraping a chalkboard. But there didn't seem to be any way out. The cat's box in the basement was still full, my father still needed help planting asparagus, and the winter windows were still up. Goby's not *that* much of a pain, so we started off, Nicky and I walking, Goby riding his Kermit the Frog Big wheel with Kermit peering over his shoulder from the back rest.

"What's this 'good cause,'" I asked Nicky, "that my mom gave me ten dollars to spend on? She has *never* given me ten dollars, not even to buy my grandmother a birthday present."

"School stuff," Nicky said, shrugging. "You know, like last year when the fifth graders got on buses and went to hear the symphony—the PTA paid."

"Very educational." I yawned, "That sounds like something my mother would think was worth ten dollars."

"You know what we get this year?"

"We learn how to rotate crops."

"Close."

"Oral hygiene lessons?"

"Right!"

"You're kidding."

"Right," She grinned at me. "This year we go on an overnight."

"Come on."

"And put a whole *school* of fish between Mr. Nagel's sheets."

"Outdoor Ed!" I yelled. "They're letting us go?" I thought after last year they were never going to have outdoor Ed again. Hiding a catfish in the principal's bed was too much that's what they said.

Nicky started walking backward in front of me. "They lied."

"The whole fourth grade? Our class and Mr. Stafford's?" I asked her. "All night long?"

"Two nights," she said, "at this camp almost ninety miles away in Wisconsin. Mom says we'll be in the big lodge place—the girls *and* the boys. And the teachers, too, I guess. Mom says they've decided we're more *mature* than last year's fourth graders.

I rolled my eyes at her. I'd been mad when I thought we weren't going, but now I wasn't so sure. I'd never been away from home in another state—not without my folks. A couple of sleepovers, sure, but . . .

"Besides," she went on, "they're sending in more chaperones. There'll be Mr. Nagel and Miss Planet and Mr. Stafford, and anybody else they can con into it, I guess."

"Hold up!" Goby called from half a block back. We held up.

He was frowning as he pedaled towards us. "My pants are wet," he said.

"That's because you've been sitting in the grass and it rained last night," I told him.

"Really?" he asked. He frowned again and turned his Big Wheel around. "I want to go home."

"You'll dry," I told him.

"You can't be homesick," Nicky explained, "We're not that far from home. Besides, Mom is at school and she needs you there holding onto her leg while she walks around the gym." We kept going.

Goby sat still for a minute, deciding. Then he honked the frog crooking horn, leaned back and cranked like crazy to catch up with us. "Zoom," he zoomed, and sped between us to wait at the corner.

When we finally got to school, Nicky opened the front door and let Goby steam down the hall like it was the Indy 500. If they caught him inside on his Big Wheel he'd wail and they'd let him off just for the quiet. If they caught me inside on my bike, I'd get life for sure with no time off for good behavior. Goby left his wheels at the gym door like a big deal who doesn't care beans if he gets a ticket.

But when we stepped inside, he turned into a little kid again. He didn't bound off and grab his mother's leg like Nicky said he would. He picked mine instead and hugged it like he was trying to squeeze toothpaste out the top. It's true that the sweaty old gym looked wild. From the ceiling hung the huge white silk parachute we sometimes use in gym class. It was swung from all four basketball hoops and it sagged low, like a cloud about to pour. Each of the hoops was covered by a nest of fuzzy brown-paper strips with a pterodactyl popped on top. While marching from class to gym the week before we'd peered through the art room door to see the sixth graders make those pterodactyls out of papermache. The bodies were purple, the bat like wings drooped, and the orange beaks opened wide, like they were ready to snap up a bellyful of little kid. Goby peeked at them from behind my knee.

"Hey Goby, we'll see you later," Nicky yelled over her shoulder, charging through clumps of parents and kids. When I tried to follow her, I had to walk like Frankenstein, dragging my Goby leg as I went.

And just as I was about to give him a fast shake, I went blind. *Zap*, just like that. These hands gripped my eyes from behind and a boy's voice said, very high, "I am a dinosaur. If you guess who I am you get a free gift."

"I don't want a free gift." I tried to pull loose, but my anchor held fast. Goby was sitting on my foot, his legs wrapped around my leg. And his pants *were* wet. I hoped it really was because he'd been sitting in the damp grass.

"Clue number one," the voice said "I have jaws like a crocodile and teeth like daggers."

"You're Sam Fox," I answered, because that's who was holding my eyes.

"Dwerp," he said, and squeezed together. I saw flashy yellow stars like Fourth of July sparklers.

"You've got to try or it isn't any fun."

Goby grabbed my hand.

"Clue number two," the high voice charged on. "I have fierce claws and I am the Brontosaurus's biggest enemy. I hold down my prey and tear the flesh off his bones."

"Sounds more like a Sam Fox all the time."

"He's an Allosaurus," Goby said from the floor. He'd learned that when Nicky and I studied for the test. It was his favourite dinosaur by far. "Al-to-saur-us," he said like he was licking on lollipop. He unwrapped himself from my foot. My sock was damp.

"Double dwerp," Sam muttered, and let go off my eyes. Goby wandered off towards a game called Tar Pits where his mother was selling tickets. I turned to see Sam's cute little Allosaurus costume, but he wasn't wearing one. He had on jeans and a sweater dotted with red hearts. His dark brown hair bounced as he and Lewis Lesley flapped their arms, waving the helium balloon tied to their wrists.

"Great costume," I told him. "Especially the jaws, claws and teeth like daggers."

Sam did not smile.

Lewis laughed until he saw Sam looking grim. "Nobody wanted to make costumes this year," he told me.

Sam shrugged. "My grandmother says dinosaurs are extinct because their shapes don't make sense. She served a whole batch of Stegosaurus capes, though for the tar Pits game."

"You want a balloon?" Lewis asked, holding his wrist out to me.

"I didn't win it."

"You knew, though we just had a test."

"No answer, no prize," Sam said, pushing Lewis aside. "Kim, you better go buy your door prize tickets. They're going to draw the winners at —." Suddenly he stopped talking, put his fingers to his lips, and pointed to the gym door. His balloons flipped through the air.

Lewis turned and tiptoed around behind Michelle Ezry, who stood facing the other end of the gym. He snuck up on her, flung his hands over her eyes, and began his memorized speech. "I am a dinosaur. If you guess who I am you get a free gift. Clue number one: I-am-the-biggest-and-heaviest-of-the-dinosaurs."

"If-you-do-not-let-my-eyes-go-I will-flip-you-and-you-will be-the flattest-of-dinosaurs," Michelle said, very calm. "You will be a dinosaur rug."

I decided Michelle could take care of herself, so I wandered around to see what I could spend Mom's ten dollars on. At the first long table somebody was painting names on barrettes. The next one had kid's high school brothers and sisters having hearts and flowers and skulls on people's cheeks and foreheads. Then there was a booth with silver star wands and little tinsel crowns, not high on the list of stuff I wanted.

Mrs. Fox, Sam's huge, half-deaf grandmother, was in charge of the bake sale table. And across the gym I could see Nicky with R.X Shea and Ruby Bougainvillea. They were trying to win goldfish in little plastic Baggies. It didn't seem like dinosaur to me, but I was about to go to win it myself as a pet for Fido when this hand with about four rings on it grabbed my shoulder. Mrs. Fox had escaped from her booth.

"I have a bunch of brownies for you, dotty," she boomed, guiding me over to the long table covered with plates of ginger bread men and chocolate chip cookies and carrot cake with white icing an inch thick. "My brownies always, *always* go first. And if your mother hadn't warned my son you were coming, I wouldn't have saved any. I've been telling people they're all sold."

I have to admit, her brownies *are* always fantastic. They are thick and rich and gooey like fudge, with chunks of walnuts in all the right places. Even piled on a paper plate covered with plastic wrap, their dark-chocolately smell leaked out and curled into my mouth.

"I thought your father was coming. Where is he?" she shouted, snapping the ten dollar bill from my hand.

"Home, I guess," I told her. She gave me eight dollars and a broken oat meal-raisin cookie in change.

"Well, sonny, have your mother and father finally stopped fighting?" she yelled. People for yards around turned slightly to listen. I wondered how she got that. Then I remembered when my mom called Sam's about the brownies. She'd said how my dad is stubborn as a mule about going to the doctor for gas pains. And now when she wanted him to go he said he didn't need to pay forty dollars to find out he eats too many cucumbers. Sam's mom must have spread the word. Mrs. Fox, though, made it sound like they were going at each other with bows and arrows.

"Pretty much," I said loud, so she could hear, but that didn't sound quite right. "It's no big deal," I went on, but people had turned away. "I've gotta go," I mumbled through a mouthful of cookie and fled to the other side of the gym. Next she'd be asking if I didn't think Sam was the cutest boy in fourth grade.

Halfway across, Goby ran up and spun around to show me the cap he was wearing.

"I won this in the Tar Pits," he said. "I got out. That's how you win." The cap was a brown cloth with a hood that reached to his eyelashes. All the way from his forehead down his back was a mountain range of scales shaped like triangles.

"What do dinosaurs say?" he asked, scraping at my jeans with his claws and aiming for my wrist with his teeth.

"Roogie-roogie," I told him, holding my arms over my head.

"Roogie-roogie," he answered. "Can I have one of your brownies? They smell good."

"No, you can't. They're poison," I said and kept walking.

"Last call for door prize tickets," a crackly voice announced on the loudspeaker. "Fifty cents a ticket, two for a dollar. Eight big prizes: a luxury weekend for two at McManderly, a weekday lunch at the Poland's, Stockton's finest food, with Miss Planet, Miss Vanilla, or our very own principal, Mr. Nagel, and more, much more. Get your razzle-dazzle, high class prize tickets here."

Nicky, R.X and Ruby were still at the goldfish booth, each of them clutching a fat Baggie of goldfish and water.

"My dad did it when he was in college," Ruby was saying.

"You lie."

"I don't either, I think there's something about it in the *Guinness Book of World Records*."

"About your dad?"

"About people swallowing goldfish." She held at her baggie. Nobody won this game. Then, after a few minutes I forced them out of that booth. We saw here and there, bought some tickets, and then on announcement came up, that the prizes of the tickets were being announced. We got collected near the booth. Till we reached the booth some prizes were already announced. The next prizes a lot of kids wanted. A week day lunch at McDonalds meant sitting on stools at the counter and ordering real hamburgers and fries while everybody at school was eating plastic lasagna. The first one was with Miss Vanilla, a really neat fifth grade teacher. Marshall Duguid in my class won that. I thought he was going to die giggling. Lunch with Miss Planet went to some kid's father. His kids were in kindergarten and second grade, so Miss Planet said if he would rather have an evening's free babysitting, she'd do that instead. The father said, "Good grief, yes."

The other lunch taker was Mr. Nagel. Mr. Nagel doesn't look like he even ate a hamburger in his real life. He wears dresses with bows at his neck and little half glasses, and his idea of a costume on Halloween in a white sunbonnet. My parents like him because they say he is "no nonsense."

"And the winner of the lunch with Mr. Nagel is . . ." Goby drew out a long string of tickets that hadn't been separated. ". . . somebody who bought a batch," Mrs. Rose announced on the speaker, "somebody who must want to have lunch with our principal pretty badly." She took the wad of tickets from Goby, beamed out at us all, and announced, "It's Kim Street!"

"Roogie-roogie," Goby said. "I should have stayed at home and cleaned the cat's box."

2

ON TRIAL

"Good morning, class," Miss Planet said, like she does every morning after the last bell.

"Good morning, Miss Planet," we answered all together, like we'd done everyday since school began.

This time after she'd checked the roll and cafeteria count and after we'd said the pledge, Miss Planet leaned back against her desk and stoned at us like she was trying to decide for sure if we were good apples or rotten.

"Well, 4B," she began, seriously, "it appears we're going to do it." It? We shot quick looks at each other and wondered. Run the mile? Skip recess forever? Teach old dogs new tricks?

"If everything goes well," she went on, "we *are* contrary to an earlier decision, going on Outdoor Education this year."

It was for sure, then. My eyes began to prickle, and woollyworms to crawl around in my stomach. There was a ripple of "Wow" in the class. Yelps of joy.

"At a cost, I might add, of only eleven-fifty per person because of Saturday's highly successful Dinosaur Delight. What do you think of that?" She smiled like she thought it was fantastic.

"I'll tell her," I thought in a flash, "that I can't afford it."

"Scholarships, of course, are available," she went on, pacing up and down in front of the chalkboard. "Now, I expect you've all heard how a few of last year's fourth graders spoiled trip for everyone with their childish, immature pranks. So, when Mr. Nagel asked me some weeks ago if I thought room 4B was ready for a nature study trip, I had to think long and hard." She rubbed her head like all that thinking had pained her. "But I told him that 4B was ready. So, three weeks from today, if you've been perfect or near perfect in every way, we and room 4A—the whole fourth grade—will spend three days at camp trotter in Wisconsin.

Three days meant two nights. Two nights away from home. In another state. My heart chuffing like I'd dashed down the hall to beat the bell, and my head swarmed with way to be a whole lot less than perfect so they'd call the whole thing off. But I kept smiling like I thought it was great. Some flags you don't wave.

"Now, I have a packet of information for each of you to take home to your parents or guardians this afternoon explaining what we plan to do in outdoor education studies and what you need to bring. I don't want any of them stuck in your lockers and forgotten."

It wouldn't do any good to leave the stuff in my locker. Parents have a way of hearing about things like that. But I *could* plan to have a stomachache.

"My grandmother has volunteered to come as a cheaper one, what with so many mothers working," Sam chirped, like he not only *knew* already about the trip, but knew *all* about it.

"The first thing we're going to do in preparation," Miss Planet said, as she erased Friday's assignments from the board, "is to change gears in science. Now that we're finished the unit on dinosaurs, this afternoon we'll be moving on to the live animals of our woods including skunks.

Everybody laughed. Skunks sound funny.

Nicky raised her hand. "Hey, we're going from extinct to stinked," she said, and everybody laughed.

Miss Planet lowered her head and looked grim.

"That, Nichola, was uncalled for." And then she smiled. "You stole my punch line. I should fine you a dollar for theft."

Nicky groaned, reached in her desk, and pulled out a bill of Monopoly money, but Miss Planet waved it away, laughing.

"In any case, it's court time," Miss Planet went on. For two whole months we'd been studying local government, and our room was set up like a town. We named it Stardom, starry for Miss Planet's kingdom, though, of course, it was *supposed* to be a democracy. Anyway, most of our desks were pushed back against the walls of the room, and each of us had masking—tape markers on the floor to show the land we owned around our desks. It was our private property. The places that weren't marked off private were streets and parks, except for Miss Planet's desk in the corner. That was City Hall, and she was the big shot.

Sam's desk was against the windows next to City Hall, then me, then Jeremy Hanna and Trace Hogrefe and Emily Hanson and Arthur Elliot. Miss Planet had tried to girl-boy-girl-boy us, but there were too many boys to make it come out right. Nicky sat across the room next to Marshall and then Michelle. Ruby was one of the kids whose desks were clumped together as apartment buildings in the big middle space we called Central Park.

Also in Central Park was the courthouse. It was a round yellow table, actually and when we had court, we put a chair on the table for the person accused of the crime. We had city council meetings and park board meetings, and we set up business and stuff, but we all liked court best. Somebody was always suing somebody for something five dollars and up for bugging, ten dollars for tripping. There was a whole list of possibilities.

"Fifteen minutes for court today, no more. That's all we can spare," Miss Planet announced.

"But we've got seventeen cases," Sam said. "That's no fair."

"Most courts have too many cases. Fifteen minutes."

"OK, court-is-in-session-order-in-the-court," Lewis said, fast as fire-crackers. He was bailiff. Sam, who was judge, sat down on the orange judge's stool. "The first case is Marshall versus Kim." He banged the gavel on the edge of the table. "Hurry up, Kim. We haven't got forever."

I climbed onto the table and sat in the chair looking out over the class like I was king of the mountain.

"Are you innocent or guilty?" Sam asked.

"Innocent," I told him. "I was framed."

"Guilty, guilty, guilty," Marshall sighed, shaking his head like he was sorry for me that I had to lie.

The rest of the class was listening only half way. Most of them were whispering or passing notes about the sleeper camp. Miss Planet was working on some papers at her desk. Emily had folded her arms on the back of her chair and was resting her head on them.

Sam shifted on the judge's stool. Around his waist he wore a belt that was printed SAM -SAM SAM . He had two barrettes from the fair that said SAM-SAM SAM on them, too. Not that anybody was going to forget. I had my baseball cap on, backward.

"What are the charges?" he asked Marshall.

"The charges are that Kim pushed me, your honor," Marshall said.

"The charge sheet says it was nine fifty-two in the morning," Lewis reported.

It had happened at nine fifty-two weeks ago, so it hardly seemed worth fighting about. But Sam had forgotten to make me promise to tell the whole truth and nothing but the truth, so I lied.

"Your honor, I didn't do it," I said.

Marshall's face turned red and he banged his fist on the table my chair sat on, and it shook. He loved going to court. He played it like a TV soap—"Your honor, she did so! You did so push me!" he yelled. "You pushed me on Michelle's land and she's suing me for trespassing." Michelle grinned and tipped her baseball cap at us.

"All I know is, I didn't, or if I did, I didn't mean it."

"You have any witness?" Sam asked him.

He had four, all boys. And so I got fined for pushing.

"I thought you might try to get out of it by using your *in*fluence," Ruby called as I handed over the money. "I mean, you're going to have lunch with the prin-cipal, aren't you? Wow-*ee*!" I could have poked her, but since I'd just gotten fined for pushing, it didn't seem right. Besides, the possibility of witnesses was pretty good. Also, the fine doubled the second time around, and my money supply was getting low.

Sam banged the gavel again. I stood up and stretched like I didn't care beans for losing two hundred dollars to Marshall and climbed down from the defendant's chair as slowly as possible.

"Next case," Sam declared and read off Jeremy versus Arthur, who had other boys to be lawyers for them.

"What did these guys do last year on Outdoor Ed that was so bad?" Emily asked me as soon as I got back to my seat. "It must have been awful."

"Just stuff," I said. "Frogs in the boy's shower stall and like that."

She leaned over to my ear. "Have you ever been far away from home at night?" she whispered.

"Lots of times," I lied. "We slept in tents and thought we heard bears in the night, and bats." I did do that once in Nicky's backyard, but it rained, so we went home to bed before midnight. "How about you?"

"Oh, sure," she said, straightening up. "Sure. Lots of times. I'm not scared of anything. I was just wondering." And she started to laugh.

"Order in the court," Lewis called. "Any more disturbances and I'll clear the room."

After Arthur was found not guilty of stealing the top of Jeremy's blue pen because half the class has blue pens just like it and who's to know whether the top on Arthur's desk was Jeremy's or not. Miss Planet gave us a spelling test of local government words. I missed munisiple . . . municipal . . . municipal.

But I was great at recess. I shine at recess. It was an excellent warm kickball recess day. And when that ball came smooth at the end of our inning, I made a crater a mile deep in it with my toe. We had two on base. R.X and Arthur. My ball sailed up, hit a cloud or two, and angled down in to the spit pit, and that meant we were all home free. It also meant I would get two points for kicking a pit ball. That made the score four to three. I strolled, very casual toward first base, a hero.

The spit pit is this disgusting staircase next to the playground that is filled with gross junk. Kids sometimes spit in it, and nobody likes to slip on all the mold getting kickballs out. So it was like somebody had waved a magic wand or something when, just as I was about to tap first base, the ball popped out of the pit. It sailed back up and onto the field like a movie playing in reverse.

Geez, I thought, there's a seal in there escaped from Lincoln Park Zoo. It's sliding down the spit pit steps, flipping balls off its nose. I didn't see how that ball could possibly have *bounced* out because the place is crammed with mud-crusted mittens and scarves, rotten bananas, and at least one three-page paper on the life and death of Tyrannosaurus case. Those things a ball would just sink its seams into.

But there it was, my pit ball back in play. I ran like crazy toward second. But, wouldn't you know, the ball was aimed straight *at* second. Marshall, who'd already won two hundred dollars from me in court, caught it and tagged me out. Just like that.

My team all started screaming and demanding a reply and calling foul and cheat. There was a lot of pushing and showing, too, until Miss Planet raised her voice. "OK, friends, what did I say about good behaviour? You keep this up and 4B will definitely *not* be long for Outdoor Ed. Think about it."

"How'd I do?" a low, old voice called from somewhere under ground level. "Didn't break anything, did I?"

We all turned again to the spit pit, but it wasn't the seal from Lincoln park zoo whose fringed bald head we saw. It was Mr. Gooseberry, the custodian. He was chuckling. "Boy, that thing shot at me like Hailey's comet." He had a black plastic sack hung over his shoulder and a shovel in his hand.

We all stood staring. "Heading straight at my head, it was. So I stepped back, wound up, and . . ." He put the bag down, grabbed the shovel with two hands, and, using it like a bat, showed us how he'd slammed the ball out of the pit. He rolled his shoulders around like it had been *some* jolt, too. Then, picking the fat bag back up and heading toward the trashroom, he said, "I am giving that stairwell a good spring cleaning. Lots of stuff blows down there during the wintertime, you know?"

The bell rang. The game was over, and my team had lost. But nobody felt like arguing about points anymore.

"That was wild," Ruby said, grabbing the kickball to take it inside. "The voice from the spit pit! Sounds like a ghost story."

"Yeah," I told her, "and my best kick of the year shoots back to haunt me. There ought to be a rule."

"Right," Ruby said. "Any pit ball returned by shovel counts triple."

"Hey, Ruby," Nicky called, catching up with us.

"I looked it up last night."

We both stared at her.

"The goldfish. I looked it up in the *Guinness Book of World Records*. And you were right. It was in there." Ruby slugged and started to hurry on ahead like she didn't want to hear.

"No kidding," Nicky went on, walking faster and catching Ruby by the elbow. "This is interesting. It says the book won't list records for 'potentially dangerous categories,' and that those are swallowing chewing gum, live ants, raw eggs in the shell, marshmallows—and goldfish."

"Marshmallows?" I asked. "What's potentially dangerous about marshmallows?"

"What's 'potentially dangerous'?" Ruby asked, her voice shaking a little.

"I think," Nicky said, as we climbed the steps back to our room on the second floor, "I think that means it *could* kill you, but not for sure."

"Marshmallows?" I asked again.

"What if it doesn't stay swallowed long?" Ruby wanted to know.

"Oh, then it's perfectly safe," Nicky told him, making it up for sure.

"Except for the goldfish," I said. "It couldn't have been very safe for the goldfish."

"Speaking of meals that won't stay down," Ruby interrupted, "when you gonna eat with fearless leader?"

"He says the day after Outdoor Ed because that's when his calendar has an empty space, but I'm gonna get out of it," I told her.

"Sounds potentially dangerous," she giggled.

"If we're late she'll kill us," Marshall was saying as he and Sam ran up the stairs behind us.

"No, she won't. She outlawed capital punishment," Sam told him, passing the three of us at a trot.

Actually, the city charter rules fined you a hundred dollars a minute for tardiness. We all made it to the room about fifty dollars after the bell. But Miss Planet didn't notice. She was standing at the front of the room talking to a handsome gentleman with thick black hair. We knew him. His name is Patrick Ivanovitch. And he is this wild substitute who taught us two days in February while Miss Planet was out with the flu. He threw a wicked snowball, square danced like an Early American, and wasn't afraid to get his feet wet. Miss Planet had to talk up to him because he is over six feet tall and she is barely five. They were smiling and laughing, though and couldn't have been thinking about us, late or not.

Mr. Ivanovitch was wearing the same bell tie he'd worn that day in February when we'd bet we could make him cry just by being awful. The tie was jingling like crazy as he laughed at something Miss Planet told him.

"Joan," he asked, raising his dark eyebrows, "will we meet before then?"

Miss Planet nodded and handed him a big manila envelope.

"Joan?" Sam whispered to me, as we sank back in our desks. "*Joan*! He called Miss Planet 'Joan!"

"That's because Joan is her name," I explained.

"I *know* Joan is her name, but how does he know it?" He shifted nervously in his seat. "I don't like this one bit. They're *friends*!"

"They're so *cueshee* together," I heard Trace tell Jeremy. The boys make up these dumb words and then use them all the time. Cueshee means "cute."

"I love his military green trousers, don't you?"

"Yeah, and she's got that, like, darling dimple, and he's so . . ."

"Tall," Sam said to them, leaning over the front of my desk. "He's much too tall for her."

"Yes, but I'm going to grow and he's not. He's as high as he's ever going to get. And he's just all wrong for her. When I grow up . . . "

"She'll be married and have two kids," Emily told him. "She must be at least twenty five years old."

Sam turned her head away, flipping his hair especially far to show how much he thought of *that* idea. He raised his hand and, when Miss Planet didn't notice, started flapping it around. The drone in the class got louder.

"Miss Planet," Sam finally demanded, "what are we supposed to be doing?"

Miss Planet stopped talking to the substitute. "My friends, you are supposed to be silent while I talk with our guest Mr. Ivanovitch, whom I think you all know."

He bobbed his head at us, his tie pinging, to let us know *he* remembered.

Mr. Ivanovitch hugged the big envelope Miss Planet had given him and said to us, "I am sorry to interrupt your lessons, but Miss Planet and I . . . " He looked up at her as though he'd just thought of something. "Miss Planet had some important papers for me. Perhaps I could tell you . . ." And he glanced upto Miss Planet to see if telling us was OK. When she nodded, he went on, "We're going to . . . "

"To get married," Sam gasped, turning to look at me in horror. As he turned, he knocked the gavel off his desk, and it clattered to the floor.

Mr. Ivanovitch, startled, reached over to pick the gavel up, stepping, as he did, inside the taped-off section of Sam's property. According to class rules, that was trespassing unless you asked permission, or were invited, or like that.

"Mr. Ivan-low-witch," Sam, said sweetly, "you probably don't know it, but you're on private property."

Mr. Ivanovitch, totally puzzled, pushed the hair out of his eyes with the handle of the gavel and looked to Miss Planet for an explanation.

"Sam," she said impatiently, "it should be perfectly clear that Mr. Ivanovitch is a visitor and . . ."

"I know," Sam told her with a little laugh, "I do apologize. It was just an automatic thing. Mr. Ivan-low-witch is an outsider. I'm sorry."

A lot of Mr. Ivanovitch's is bounce had disappeared, and he looked as though he wasn't sure he wanted to go on. But he took a deep breath and did.

"We are going to go on a trip together," he continued, skipping over Sam and smiling out at the rest of the class. He spread both his arms wide. Sam groaned. "All of us. Miss Planet and Mr. Nagel have asked me to go with you to Wisconsin to learn about nature." He glanced back at Sam and smiled. "Isn't that wonderful!"

"Wonderful," Sam muttered, and, leaning back in his chair, he narrowed his eyes and folded his arms tight. "Just wonderful."

3

IF ONE OF THOSE BOTTLES SHOULD HAPPEN TO FALL

Sometimes, three weeks seems like forever, but these three whipped past so fast I didn't have time to catch a cold or sprain a toe. On the morning we were supposed to leave for camp I still hadn't made up a really good reason to stay home. Mom refused to buy my fever or sore throat. She took my temperature and made me say Ah-ah-h-h-h. My father growled from the bedroom that he had a bellyache, and when I said I did too, she opened the front door and waved me out. "Kim Street, it's going to be a terrific trip," she said. I walked halfway down the steps and looked back at her without smiling.

That's when I saw the cat streak out between her legs. Fido's an indoor cat, so I rushed over to trap him under the bushes.

"Leave him to me," she said. "The Ryders are ready to leave." So, even though my throat felt like it really might start to hurt at any minute, I climbed into the Ryder's car with my suitcase.

That's how I ended up at school marching to the camp bus at nine-fifteen, *laughing*, wondering if anybody else was dying to stay at home.

Mrs. Ryder and the other mothers waved as we filed past. Two or three had babies strapped to their chests in Kangaroo pouches. Goby was there, too.

"I want to go," he wailed. "I want to put a shark in Mr. Nagel's sleeping bag." He yanked his mother forward by the knee of her jeans. "That was *last* year," Mrs. Ryder explained calmly. Then she reached over and stretched a wool cap over my head.

"Your mother said to give this to you at the last minute so you wouldn't leave it behind," she told me. "And you're to wear it so you're sure to be well for your lunch with Mr. Nagel on Thursday."

Goby howled. "This year," she explained to him "they're going to be good at camp. You'll be happier at home."

It took two school buses to hold fifty-one kids with their duffles and suitcases. We had so many bags it looked like we were off for a year in Australia. Three kids stayed home sick. Nicky said they were just scared to leave their teddy bears. I laughed and laughed, and my woollyworms started doing gymnastics in my stomach.

"Michelle, hold still!" Michelle stopped, embarrassed, and faced her mother's camera. Then she grabbed the guys around her and made us stay too. "OK, all four of you, smile!" she said.

Nicky held two fingers up behind Michelle's head like they were horns. I stood totally in back of Nicky except for one leg and one arm, which I struck out so it looked like Nicky had three of each. R.X shoved one side of his face up and pulled the other down like it was made of Silly Putty.

Mrs. Ezry laughed and clicked the shutter.

"Well, there's the Before picture. When you get back I'll take an after. Be good, now," she called as we climbed up the steps.

Nicky and I sat in the second row of the front bus. The back bus had Mr. Stafford in it with his 4A's and Miss Glass, their student teacher from National College of Education. Mr. Nagel and Mrs. Fox were driving all the way to Camp Trotter so there'd be a car in case of emergency, and, I think, so they wouldn't have to ride with us.

Everyone was on our bus but Mr. Ivanovitch, who stood searching up and down the sidewalk both ways like he was about to cross the street in heavy traffic, only there weren't many cars coming. He wore purple check shirt, jeans that had a few miles worn on them, and hiking boots with major scars.

Miss Planet opened the window by her seat in the middle of the bus. "Come aboard," she called to him. "We're ready to roll."

He took a step back and checked behind both buses, then shifted his feet like he wasn't sure he wanted to leave.

Miss Planet called again. "We're all here," she said, "and accounted for."

Sam, who was sitting one row ahead and across the aisle from her, poked Lewis, who was next to him. "They're going to fight," he giggled.

"Maybe he's going to chicken out," Nicky said, turning around in her seat and laughing with him.

"He knows us." I laughed too. It felt pretty good to be laughing at someone.

So when Mr. Ivanovitch finally climbed on the bus and the driver swooshed the doors closed, we were all breaking up over funny, purple, late Mr. Ivanovitch.

He sat next to Miss Planet, stuffing his fancy pouch under the seat, but she didn't bark at him for being late. She smiled.

As we pulled away, mothers called goodbye and Goby stood in his tiptoes, waving like crazy. Mrs. Ezry took a picture of the bus.

"Let's sing," Jeremy yelled from the back.

"Let's not," Ruby called from the front. Miss Planet and Mr. Ivanovitch started talking. Joan and Patrick. "Sam's jealous," Arthur said from the seat across from us.

"I am not," Sam leaped forward, whispering.

"I just happen to think he is totally wrong for her. They'd never ever be happy."

Mr. Ivanovitch and Miss Planet broke into this huge hysterical guffaw like one of them had told the all-time funny joke. Then Mr. Ivanovitch opened his flowery pouch and offered her a mint, and she took it.

Sam sank down in his seat. Nicky and I laughed out aloud.

"You're absolutely right, Sam," Lewis said, looking straight over at me. "They'd probably fight and end up getting divorced. It happens all the time. Marshall's parents are divorced. So are Ruby's. Mine are even thinking about it. It happens *all* the time." And it seemed like he was talking to me. I wondered what he knew.

The bus was rolling past my house. Was he talking about my folks? I stood up and wondered what I could do so they'd let me off.

"Down in front," Marshall said, and I sat. It could be that those ladies at the fair knew something I didn't. They smiled like they felt really sorry for me. I felt sorry for me too.

In the back of the bus they were singing:

There was an old man named Michael Finnegan.
He had whiskers on his chinnegan.
Along came the wind and blew them in again.
Poor old Michael Finnegan.

Begin again. And they began again. And again.

I began to wonder if I'd left my bike outside.

I *might* have. If I did and my folks were getting a divorce, they wouldn't see it out there turning to rust. There were clouds and it looked like rain.

I was half listening as Nicky and R.X and Michelle started to sing.

Ninety-nine bottles of beer on the wall,
Ninety-nine bottles of beer.

Mr. Ivanovitch jumped up and rushed over. "Oh, my dears, don't," he said. "I can't travel all the way to Wisconsin in a busful of broken beer bottles. How about ninety-nine cans of pop?"

"It won't sell," R.X said. "Bottles of gin?"

He rolled his eyes. "Cartons of milk, may be?"

"Pitchers of spit?" Nicky suggested

"Oh, good grief," he laughed, turning back to Miss Planet. "I give up."

If one of those pitchers should happen to fall
Ninety-five pitchers . . .

When I sang with them my flip-flopping woollyworms dozed, and I decided this was going to be fun after all.

Ruby read signs out loud: "WOW Exotic Dancers," "FM100, a beautiful Place to be," "Great America Theme Park, Second Right," "Filling Station Restaurant, Fabulous Food," "You are leaving Illinois, Land of Lincoln."

But we were still less than an hour away from school when Emily hurried up from the back of the bus, tugged on Mr. Ivanovitch's shirt, and said, "When are we going to be there?"

"Oh, ages," he told her. "We're not even halfway. We'll be there in about ninety minutes."

"I don't feel so good," she whispered, and he got up and followed her to the back of the bus.

As soon as he left, Sam moved over to Mr. Ivanovitch's seat.

"How about a page or two of Mad Libs, Miss Planet?" he asked.

"I'm gone," she told him. "Shoot."

Sam smiled over at us. "Adjective?"

"Peaceful," she said with a sign.

After we'd stopped at the side of the road for Emily to get sick in the bushes, we started passing more plane hills than billboard ones. There was a huge black bird sitting in the top of a tree with no leaves, a pick-your-own-strawberries farm that was closed because it wasn't strawberry season yet, great green lakes around almost every curve, and lots of black-and-white cows that Marshall said were cueshee and Arthur said were Holsteins.

"What are we going to do up there?" Michelle came over and asked Nicky. "I mean *do*. Last year's fourth grade got famous for Outdoor Ed. You want to plan ahead or shall we just make it up as we go along?"

Nicky reached into the small paper bag she'd brought on the bus and opened it up a crack so Michelle and I could look inside. A hairy, warty, gangrene-gray rubber hand lay limp in the bottom of the sack, ready to pick up and wave at night through somebody's open window. I felt like it was already dark, and I wished I was home with my blue striped sheets pulled over my head. And my mom and dad listening to the *Late Evening News*. And then I remembered that my dad hadn't said goodbye and that the cat was lost and my bike dead and stolen. My hands began to sweat.

Beep-beep-beep-beep-beep—beep-beep! The bus driver honked to announce we had arrived at Camp Trotter. The sun was shining now, and the cap I'd forgotten I was wearing was much too hot.

"I'm starving," R.X. called as the bus ground to a stop. "It's eleven thirty-seven. When do they feed us?"

We climbed out and gathered around while the driver opened the back door of the bus and handed out bags. Trace, the littlest kid in our class, had a suitcase with wheels on it. He tried to pull it along the gravel by its strap, but it fell over on its side like a stubborn dog. My things were in a little red suitcase of my mothers. You could tell those kids who'd been to camp before they had scruffy duffles that looked like they'd been stored in cans.

I followed Miss Planet up the steps to the long stone building we'd be staying. She was carrying two suitcases—hers and his. At the landing she picked some guy's underwear off the tip of the camp trotter sign, dropped it in the trash barrel, and barked, straight at me, "Don't get any ideas, my friend."

"Where are we going now?" Emily asked, looking pale still.

"I don't know," Michelle said, resting her long Khaki duffel on the lodge's pouch railing.

"But I gotta get there fast. It feels like I've got two dogs and a cat in here."

Even though they'd shown us a map and told us ahead of time who we were roaming with and where, it was a mad house inside. Mr. Ivanovitch had rushed ahead of the mob and was stationed in the front hall, handing everybody who came in two white sheets, a pillowcase, and a towel. "I want to see snappy hospital corners on your beds," he told us all. Miss Glass next to him, shouted out room numbers to people who'd forgotten. I went searching for room nine.

"Hey, you guys," Ruby yelled, tramping down the steps. "Room nine is next to the boy's shower. A room with a view. Can you believe it?"

"Don't believe it," Mr. Ivanovitch called. "Upstairs is the boys floor. Girls are downstairs."

As we headed into the real room nine, Ruby and I bumped into Nicky rushing out. "I'm not going to sleep in that smelly place," she said, brushing past us. "I'm going to complain." When we walked in and looked around, I thought it smelled good, damp and musty, like our basement after a good rain.

The room was small, with two dressers and two double-decker beds, a blanket folded on each. Nicky's stuff was piled on one of the top bunks. I threw my red bag on top of the other. Ruby sat down on the bed under Nicky's and sank about eight inches.

"What's a hospital corner?" she asked. I climbed on my top bunk and tried to fold the sheet, sharp corners like my dad had made in the Army and taught me how. Except I wonder how people make top bunks. With my suitcase and my feet at one end, I spread out the sheet and tucked in the corner, crawled to the other end, pushed the suitcase behind me and tried to pull the sheet straight. But I was on top of it and it wouldn't pull. When I tried jumping in the air and yanking at the same time, all I did was bang my head on the ceiling. My bed looked like a plate of spaghetti.

"Doesn't look so great from underneath," Ruby said. "Look, don't tell anybody, but I never made a bed before."

"Well, then, don't worry about hospital corners." I hopped down and tried to stuff the sheets in any old way. "It's no big deal."

"Room check in ten minutes," Miss Planet shouted as she walked down the hall. "I want those beds so I can bounce a quarter on them."

"Why should she want to bounce a quarter on a bed?"

"To show it's light like a trampoline. That's supposed to be good. My dad says . . . " I told her, and suddenly remembered that my dad had hardly eaten or said anything at supper the night before, and he's a big eater and a big talker. I didn't know why. I hadn't figured it out before Lewis said her folks were talking about a divorce. I never knew *that* before, either—probably, I decided, there were a lot of things I didn't know.

"I've got to call home," I said "I forgot something."

"That's against the rules," Ruby told me. "what'd you forget?"

It was twelve fifteen and nobody would be home anyway except the cat, and he was probably somewhere in Ohio crying in the top of a tree. I shrugged. "I guess it's no big deal."

"They *all* smell like this," Nicky said, rushing in and vaulting onto her bed. "We'll just have to open the windows."

Emily dragged her suitcase in, plunked her things on the bed under nine, and went silently to work while Ruby watched her spread, tuck and fold.

"I never made a bed before," Ruby explained to Emily and Nicky. "Don't tell anybody." I think she wanted us to feel sorry for her and make it ourselves.

"Well, you better do it now or Miss Planet will send you home," Nicky told her.

"Really?" Emily asked brightly, dumping her pillow back out of its case.

"No, not really, but we can't eat till they're made, and I'm starved. "I watched her stuff the hairy hand and a flashlight under her pillow.

Ruby spread her sheets and blanket kitty-corner on her bed, tucked some in, and then pulled a bag of stuff out of her suitcase and set it on the crumpled blanket.

"You want to seem clever?" Ruby asked us. "I decided to beat last year's guys and their fat-fish-in-the-bed trick. You know that list they gave us, 'Articles to Bring' and 'Articles to be Left at Home'?" She whipped it out and said proudly, "I brought *all* the Articles to be Left at Home."

She waved a cellophane-wrapped package of peanut butter and crackers at us. "Number One Food." Then she opened up a small sack and poured out a heap of Hubba Bubba. "Number

Two Gum." She turned a switch on something that looked exactly like a Pepsi can, only it crackled with a static and faint echo of music. "Fine. Money." She flipped two quarters onto the bed. They didn't bounce. "And I'm counting the plastic spread in the peanut butter and crackers as number six. The only thing I didn't bring was number seven, a tape recorder, because I don't actually have one. Good stuff, huh?"

We were still deciding how to answer that when Miss Planet blasted through the door. "What ho!" she said. "This may well be the messiest room on my beat. And what's more, I believe I see an entire stack of contraband. I shall confiscate it and return it to its rightful owner when we arrive home." She scooped it up and dumped it all into its original sack. "Yours, I presume, Ruby?"

"Mine, Miss Planet," she signed.

An enormous crackly laugh rang out as a bell from the mess hall down the bill called us to lunch. It was Mrs. Fox's laugh. And it was close by.

"Oh, I'll keep an eye on them. Don't you worry," she was saying. "they won't put anything, *anything* over me." And she crackled again. Mrs. Fox was in the room next to ours, no doubt about it. On the girls' floor—Mrs. Fox was keeping her eye on *us*.

4

RIP

"Yuck, this stuff looks like imitation Central School food," Trace groaned as he plopped the bowl of Macaroni Casserole on our table. He wore a white chef's cap, which meant he was our table's "hopper," the one who goes to the kitchen for food.

"It looks like a lovely dish," Mr. Nagel said when it was passed to him, still untouched. He lifted a heaping spoonful onto his plate. There was probably fun in it. For sure there was celery.

"That's what I meant," Trace said.

"Lovely."

Dishes of chocolate pudding and a plate of carrot sticks were already on the table when we sat down, so most people ate pudding first, even though Mr. Nagel pointed out that it wasn't a good appetizer.

"Pass the peanut butter, jelly, and bread," R.X called when Trace arrived with them. He had to go back for thirds for the peanut butter and jelly, and R.X must have eaten a whole loaf bread. But the casserole just sat there with one cave in it. Even Mr. Nagel didn't take second helping. I couldn't swallow anything. The fuzzy creatures in my stomach had taken up dancing.

"Hey, Kim," Ruby whispered from the next table, "you practising up for your fancy schmancy lunch Thursday?" She pointed at Mr. Nagel and laughed behind her hand. Big deal.

Out of the mess hall windows we could see across Lake Lindalomas and the rows of big old houses on the other side. Two orange pontoon boats bobbed in the waves at the dock. I guess it was too early for water skies.

Soon Miss Planet stood up, raised her hand, and shouted, "OK, friends. I can't talk unless everybody is listening. So let's cease conversation."

At the next table Sam stopped nibbling carrot sticks long enough to lean over and ask Mr. Ivanovitch, "Have you ever noticed how mean Miss Planet can be? It's something you realize the longer you know her. She's basically a very mean person."

"OK, friends," Miss Planet went on, "when you finish, pass your plates to the hopper, who'll clean the table." Groans from the hoppers. Laughs from everyone else. "Those of you who are laughing will get your chance. And when you get back to your room make sure your bed is well made, because you'll want to collapse in it when we come back from the cemetery. It's a long way."

"Cemetery? Is she kidding?" a kid from 4A asked me. Mr. Nagel stared her down. Miss Planet had warned us about the walk to the cemetery.

"And make sure you go to the bathroom. There aren't any toilets along the way to the graveyard."

Nicky and I were the first ones out. We ran from the mess hall by the lake back to the lodge and swept through the boys's rooms upstairs, where we saw pink rabbits, Paddington bears, little heart pillows, one large stuffed donkey, a gray cat with a red ribbon, and a nightshirt printed with "Numero Uno."

Rushing down the steps before the teachers or Mrs. Fox came, we climbed fast into our top bunks so if they said, was it you on the boys's floor, we'd say, No, I'm asleep. Nobody asked, so we played catch with the hairy rubber hand until it was time to leave.

Mrs. Fox and Mr. Nagel didn't go with us to the cemetery. As we left, I heard Mrs. Fox shout to Mr. Nagel, "I'm glad I'm not going with them right after lunch. When they eat, all the juices go straight to their little stomach, you know, leaving their brains completely empty. Completely empty. It's a scientific fact."

The cemetery was almost a mile away, and we set off down the side of the road single file, in four big groups, each group with a teacher type leader. Mine got Mr. Ivanovitch. Or he got us, I'm not sure which. He called our group the Scotch Tape because, he said, he wanted us to stick together. That's better than being called the Lindalomas, which is what Mr. Stafford's was. Miss Planet's kids named themselves the CIA, for Central Intelligence Agency, and Miss Glass's group was the Bowls. Seven of the Scotch Tape were from Miss Planet's class! Nicky, Michelle, Emily, Sam, Lewis, Arthur and me. The others were 4A: Lynd, Elvis, Cyrus, Stephanie, Vinny and Grey.

About seven hundred fifty years later we got there. Two dogs had snarled at us, and a black-and-white cat followed us when we said, "Here, kitty, kitty." I wondered who Fido had followed. Mr. Stafford passed word back that if we touched the flags on the outdoor mail boxes we would be committing a federal offence and probably spend six to eight months in the penitentiary. And Lewis's new shoes had rubbed blisters on his heels, so the scotch tape had to walk slow to keep back with him.

Mr. Ivanovitch kept jogging ahead and waiting.

"Come on, Tape," he called from the cemetery gate.

"These folks can't hurt you . . ."

Emily sat down inside the entrance and refused to budge.

It was spooky. Dark clouds were rolling over, and so was a thin layer of fog. We crept slowly around, trying to fill in all the blanks on the mimeographed sheets they'd given us asking who was buried in the oldest graves and which stones were made of granite, which of sandstone, and whether there were families that died all at once. There was one—the Threadlings whose last dates were all June 14, 1879, only it didn't say why. Stars stood for people who were killed in wars.

And there was a baby angel on a gravestone, a cherub Mr. Ivanovitch liked. The stone read "Luella Wilson, Died April 4, 1858, 3 weeks, 4 days old." Mr. Ivanovitch sat in front of it and called, "Joan, this is the one I want to do a rubbing of. This one will be perfect for our new hall."

"Aha," Nicky said. "Our new hall."

Miss Planet gathered all four groups around and handed out big sheets of white paper black crayons. Mr. Stafford explained how to rub the crayon flat on the paper to get the gravestone's picture to appear. I'd done it before lots of times, rubbing a pencil over a paper-covered penny, so I knew what he was talking about.

Mr. Ivanovitch told us not to get crayon on the gravestones and set to work on his champ. When Nicky and I said we didn't know what to rub, he told us to find letters from different tombstones and spell our own names. But that got to be pretty eerie when we thought about it.

We had sat down on to humps that were dead people when Nicky spotted Sam and Lewis heading our way. We hid behind big stones marked Beucher, making ourselves as small as possible and quiet as corpses. Balancing on our toes, we waited, ready to leap out and grab them by the ankles as they passed.

But just at the instant we were going to pounce we got grabbed ourselves—by the ribs. Marshall and Jeremy had seen us hide and crept up as silent as Indians. We weren't afraid, of course, it's that when you get grabbed by the ribs, you naturally yell.

But they wouldn't let it go. "Scared cat, dirty rat, don't know what you're looking at!" They danced like spirits in the night, waving their rubbings and hauling like werewolves. And just then the wind whipped up the rain in little misty drops. We could hear it on the leaves before we felt it. I zipped my jacket up and half wished I hadn't left my cap in the room.

"Look at this," Mr. Ivanovitch said proudly, his hair blowing like a big black bush around his head. He held up his rubbing of the angel, and it was good. He hadn't moved the paper as he rubbed like we did, so nothing was smudged. You could see the baby's smile, and all the letters were clear. "Hold this for me while I get organized, will you?" he asked, handing up the rubbing and scrambling to his feet.

I grabbed and Nicky grabbed and we both got it. I got one half and she got the other. The damp paper split right down the middle.

Mr. Ivanovitch's face lost all its joy, and we knew that our "I'm sorry" weren't going to help.

"*Why* did you have to do that!" he said, tilting his head both ways to look at the damage. "I *really* wanted it and I was pleased with the funny grin the angel had and . . ." He tried to pull his hair back from the wind. Nicky gave him her half of the rubbing. He shrugged, rolled it up, and stuffed it into his raincoat pocket.

I was going to hand him my half too, but a blast of wind lifted the paper away, flipped it past an evergreen, and plastered it flat against Albert, son of M and S Matfield, died April 5, 1849.

"Oh, just toss it in the trash," he said, and ran to join the other teachers. I felt awful. He was really mad. When Mr. Ivanovitch showed them the torn paper, Miss Planet put her hand on his shoulder and looked really pained. She didn't turn to chew us out, though, so he must not have told her how it happened.

The boys went crazy when she touched him.

Mr. Ivanovitch and Miss Planet walked together on the way back, a row of boys lived up to trail behind them. Nobody cared about groups anymore.

Arthur stopped, picked up a long stick from the side of the road, and wrote in the damp dirt, "P.I + J.P" Jeremy, who was walking with him, drew a heart around it.

"She's short and he's tall," Sam announced.

"She's blonde and he's got black curly hair. She's nice and he's dwarfy. Their children would be freaks."

"*My* father's blond and *my* mother's brunette," Jeremy said.

"That's what I meant," Sam answered, shuffling through the heart like he was doing a war dance.

I rolled the torn angel up with the rubbing I'd made of my name. "Think we could stick it together with tape?" I asked Nicky.

"You got any?"

I shrugged. "He said he wanted it for his new hall, too."

"*Our* new hall, that's what it was. And who do you think 'our' is?" she asked with a grin like she knew who.

"You mean you think he *is* going to marry Miss Planet?"

"Looks like it. She carried his suitcase."

"That's because he had to run ahead to hand out sheets and towels."

"May be," she said, shrugging her shoulders.

"You know what I think we ought to do?" she asked. "I think we ought to make another rubbing for him—for them." One of the dogs who'd growled at us on the way ran up to sniff our feet. "Would they let us go back to the cemetery now?"

"No, its going to rain, too hard." The sky rumbled as if to say, that's right, fella.

"Tomorrow?"

"They've got stuff for us to do all day."

"Tomorrow night?"

"In the dark?"

"It gets dark at night."

"We could take turns rubbing. And give it to them as a wedding present."

"We'd better take a good look around at how to get there if we're going to go back at night." It was one straight road. No way to get lost.

We were the last of the line. Even Lewis and his blisters had moved on ahead because he was carrying his shoes.

The black-and-white cat padded up behind us going. "Me-owl. Me-owl."

Nicky kneeled down to it and said, "No, dummy, you no *owl.* Owls go hoot in the night. You *cat.*"

"Me-owl," it said again, not believing Nicky for a minute.

I scratched the cat's neck the way Fido liked me to do, then picked it up and carried it back to the lodge under my jacket. It was warm and had a purr so loud it sounded like it ran on batteries.

As we got to the porch the sky filled with a white-blue flash, and the thunder began to rumble through our bones. Miss Glass, who was in charge of a crate of apples in the big front hall, handed us one each. In their rooms kids were talking and laughing.

We bit into our apples and listened for a minute at the bottom of the boy's steps. If we'd really wanted to, we could have dashed to the top like we had after lunch. Miss Glass was leaning out the front door, taking deep breaths of the electric air and watching the storm move in. We could have. But didn't. Instead, I opened my jacket and let loose on the boys one black-and-white cat who thought he was an owl.

5

ZAP

The rain held off, with the clouds growling lot but not biting, so they marked us back outside to play matching games with a batch of rocks that all looked the same to me. Sam matched his granite with my granite, which I thought for sure was quartz. And then we played kickball two games at a time on a wide, open field with no fences. The ball kept lifting off and drifting away with the wind, no matter how it was thrown or kicked, and Mr. Ivanovitch made two freak home runs. Back at our playground a ball couldn't go spinning off like that into the middle distance. But then, at school, teachers didn't play kickball, either.

If we'd been at school, really, it would have been out and I would have been at home watching TV before supper. Camp Trotter didn't have a TV. For me I wouldn't have been matching roles with Sam Fox or listening to Lewis talk about how this darling lost cat took a flying leap into his upper bunk.

The later it got, the more like home it wasn't.

"Icky chicken," Trace said when R.X who was supper hopper, brought a bowl of it to our table. Trace said he never ate green beans because they gave him a rash, and he took only a mound of mashed potatoes, which he raked with his fork. Some birds who had treated much like an art project wolfed down supper. Graveyards and ground balls make you hungry. I even ate some, trying not to think about night ahead. R.X, though, was gross. She stuffed whole pieces of bread into her mouth and chewed puff-cheeked, yawning now and then to make the kids across from her sick. When Mr. Nagel looked, she always tried to have her mouth shut and her eyes staring up at the ceiling, innocent.

"R.X, I can't believe you eat this way at home," Mr. Nagel told her. She smiled, her lips sealed.

After supper some of us walked down to the lake and tried skipping a few stones—granite, marble, rubies, whatever. The waves, pushed high by the wind, ate all the stones before the third skip, even Michelle's, and she threw like a pro.

On the way back to the lodge the rain began to fall sideways, because the guts were so strong. We ran, crunching pebbles under our feet.

When the hoppers were all back from cleaning and scrubbing the tables, we gathered in the big recreation room upstairs on the boys's floor. One wall was a window looking out over the lake. Another was stone-wall—stone probably—with a fireplace in it filled with logs that weren't burning.

Mr. Stafford was showing off a batch of the day's rubbings. But a lot of kids were rolling around on the floor, shrieking, so he and Miss Planet tried to organize us into our groups again. They made us sit with no talking at all for me whole minute by the clock on the wall. Miss Glass grinned like it was really funny, but a minute is a long time. The clock said seven-seventeen when we could open them again. In the first fifteen seconds I thought about how my bike was out in the back of my house, rushing away to crust. In the second fifteen seconds I could see Fido soaked to the skin, crying for me. By thirty seconds I was watching my mother wave goodbye forever to my father, an umbrella keeping the lightning away. The mashed potatoes in my stomach had turned to plaster.

It was getting dark.

Mr. Ivanovitch, Mr. Nagel, and Mrs. Fox hurried into the room together. Mr. Ivanovitch and Mr. Nagel could tell what was going on. Mrs. Fox couldn't hear the silence.

"Well, Patrick," he bellowed, "I'm so happy for you. We're *all* so happy for you."

Mr. Ivanovitch turned red and sank to the floor with the Scotch tape. Mrs. Fox had changed into new very blue jeans and a sweat-shirt that said Iowa State. She settled herself on the flowered sofa against the wall across from the fireplace. Mr. Nagel, still in his red suit with the little striped bow at the neck, sat with her.

"Why do you suppose we're all supposed to be so happy for Mr. Ivanovitch?" Nicky asked with a grin.

"Because he had no cavities at his last checkup," I told her.

Other people were whispering the same question, but nobody asked Mr. Ivanovitch. Instead the boys, except for Sam and Lewis, all rearranged themselves on the floor until they got Mr. Ivanovitch next to Miss Planet. It wasn't all that easy to do, either, because a nature person from Camp Trotter was trying to wade through us holding a projector over his head like we were water that would ruin it. He was going to be our evening class.

"OK, you guys. Coming through. Coming through," he growled. "Let's see a little consideration here. Can't you keep this kid quiet?" he called to Miss Planet, even though we weren't making all that much noise. Mostly it was whispering. Miss Planet looked like she'd half a mind to send the guy to the principal for a good chewing out. But she stopped fuming and grinned when Mr. Ivanovitch whispered something in her ear. Sam moved in closer.

We waited on the floor in the half dark while the guy with the slides got plugged in. The exit signs glowed red in front of us. Before long the nature person was telling us what the Old Greeks thought about the sky and about constellations but out of the window behind him all we could see was thick black stripes across murky grey. There were no stars.

When the slide show started, Ruby stuck her hands up to make a rabbit on the screen. Miss Planet sent her to sit on the sofa, sandwiched between Mrs. Fox and Mr. Nagel. Everybody laughed except Ruby.

The guy finished his first round of slides with a picture of an astronaut's footsteps on the moon. He was putting another set in the projector when a blast of lightening exploded like somebody taking our picture with a giant flash cube. The thunder cracked so fast that the bolt must have grazed the window. The air smelled funny.

A lot of people yelled. Emily, who was sitting in front of Mr. Nagel's knees, started to cry. He leaned over and talked close to her ear.

Miss Planet got up, stepped over the kids around her, and flicked on the lights.

"Intermission," she said, easy, as though nothing had happened.

"Everybody stretch."

"Now, don't you worry, children," Mrs. Fox shouted as she rose from the sofa." It never strikes twice in the same place. Never and that's a scientific fact."

The lightning blinded us again.

Its blast followed before I could count one.

"Did you know there's a restaurant on the moon?' Mr. Ivanovitch asked as we were all sitting down again. I glanced at the guy with the slides, who looked annoyed.

"Why, no, Mr. Ivanovitch," Nicky answered.

"Tell us about the restaurant on the moon!"

"Well," he said, waiting till everything but the night was quiet, "it has great food, but absolutely no atmosphere." Some kids laughed, some groaned, some asked other kids next to them what it meant, but the awful, scary feeling was gone.

And that's when the lights went out. Even the red exit lights.

Everybody screamed. The room sounded like a roller coaster halfway down its first fall.

"OK, pull it back together," Miss Planet shouted.

Mr. Ivanovitch stood up. And when the howls hit bottom, she asked, "Do you all have flashlights in your rooms?" Most of us did. They were on the Articles to Bring list.

So when the projector guy headed out to fix the plug, or whatever, Mr. Nagel and Miss Glass stuck around to hush us, and the rest of the adult types went out flashlight hunting.

They weren't gone long. Each one had two for good measure.

"I expect this is really all we'll need," Mr. Ivanovitch was saying as they came in. "After all, we're not having a supermarket grand opening."

We huddled together like it was cold, listening to the blasts outside. The sky had gone crazy.

"Actually," Miss Planet told us, raising her voice over the sound effects," we were going to turn the lights out anyway."

I could hear Emily breathing raspy in her throat. Ruby had slid off the sofa when Mrs. Fox and Mr. Nagel left. She moved in close to Nicky and me.

"You know we're been talking about animals of the woods in school? Well," Miss Planet said, "most mammals—about eighty-five percent of all mammals—are awake and roaring at night."

"Geez," Ruby whispered. What a bore. "Do we have to learn *all* the time?"

"How do they find each other in the dark?" Miss Planet asked.

The night outside turned day again, but this lightning was farther away than the last.

"That's how," a kid yelled, and everybody laughed.

"Very bright," Miss Planet said. She stuck the flashlight under her chin so it made shadows on her face like she was the Teacher Monster.

"Lightning bugs flicker," a boy said.

"And do it without thunder," the teacher Monster nodded.

"Crickets make noises," another voice said.

"Very sound." She flashed her beam over the group, looking for more answers.

"Dogs smell stuff out," Marshall called.

Miss Planet aimed her light at him.

"So do sharks," Ruby yelled, and the flash landed on her. "They smell blood in the water."

"True," Miss Planet said. "Even in the dark." She snapped off her light.

The lightning had stopped, but it was still raining. There were probably no sharks in Lake Lindalomas. And the water hadn't gotten deep enough for them to snap at the windows anyway.

The other teachers and Mrs. Bosco turned off their flashlights, and we talked about how we would find each other blind.

"There were predators out there now, animals searching for food, for their prey. Each one must be careful not to be caught. We are going to play a game in the dark called Predator-Prey." I got goose bumps on my arms.

The adults, holding turned on flashlights, moved through the kids, handing out stuff. Some kids got sandpaper blocks to scrape together like in rhythm bands. Some got penlights to flash. Ruby had a kleenex soaked in perfume that smelled like roses, and Mr. Ivanovitch gave me a baby food jar with some stones in it.

"OK, you guys," Miss Planet explained, "there are four kinds of prey in this game: scrapers, lights, rattles and roses."

"What's this?" a kid called.

"That's my perfume, sonny," Mrs. Fox said from the sidelines.

"As soon as one rattler finds another rattler, one rose another rose, and so forth, both are safe," Miss Planet went on. "When you've found another creature like you, move close to a wall and sit down out of everybody's way. You are the prey." That was me—a rattler.

"OK, but four of you out there were wearing black T-shirts. You are the predators, out for your evening meal. One of you eats only the rose creatures, and so forth. When your predators meet one of your prey, tap him—or her—on the shoulder, say 'Zap' in her ear . . . "

"Or his," Sam said. "And you've made your kill."

"Exactly."

Next to me Emily was pulling a predator shirt on over her head.

In the total dark and almost total silence, we mixed ourselves up in the room, like stuffed cards. Some kids, you could tell, were holding onto each other, cheating.

"Do you think she'll kiss him?" I heard Jeremy whisper to somebody as he passed. "It's romantic in the dark."

"It is not romantic," Sam answered. "Besides, she'd probably miss. He's such a Giant."

"Predators, I hope you're ready." Miss Planet announced from over near the door. "Your prey are about to start roaming through the night woods. I'm going to give you sixty seconds in the dark." She turned a penlight on her wrist watch. "Ready. Set. *Go*!"

We whirled around sniffing, shaking, scraping and blinking. I caught onto somebody who rattled at me. It was Michelle, and we collapsed near the fireplace, glad not to be eaten. When the sixty seconds were up, the teachers turned on all eight flashlights. And we saw that nine kids had been captured. Five of them were flashlights. Two were scrapers. Two were perfume. Not a single rattler had been caught. Emily was the rattle predator. I guess they made her one to make her feel strong. But it didn't work

"Hey, Emily," Ruby yelled, "You're a real tiger." And played a few more times with different predators. "Zap!" you'd hear in the dark and "Zap!" again. Kids got smarter about not flashing lights too long and all, but anybody who'd ever had the perfumed Kleenex smelled like it the whole time.

As we dropped the stuff into cardboard boxes and sat down again, Mr. Ivanovitch lit the logs in the fireplace. The twigs began to crackle. It was scary on the total dark, but lonelier when the fire has burning. I missed home again. And nobody else seemed to be jumpy but Emily.

Mrs. Fox stepped up next to the fireplace. Now she was wearing a huge grey sweater with big humpy pockets over her Towa State sweatshirt. She leaned toward us. "I am going to tell you a tale," she said, slow and mysterious. The fire was so bright you could see almost the whole room. It was reflected in the windows, so there were two fires and two Mrs. Fox.

"Once," she began, "in the deep, dark past, there was a monkey's paw." And she told us this really bizarre story about a guy who got ground up in a machine at work because his parents wished for money with this magic monkey's paw. First they wished for two thousand dollars or something, and the insurance money for his getting ground up was two thousand dollars, so they got their money, only then they did want Monkey's paw to bring him back to life. Only when he came back that night he was still all ground up, so they had to use up their third wish to get him dead again because how are you going to sit down with your family for supper if you're all ground up? Actually, it was a gross and excellent story. And even though she is Sam's grandmother, she did a good job of telling it.

But when she announced that she is going to tell another, Mr. Nagel said, "Oh, no, I think one ghost story is quite enough tonight." He probably thought it would keep us awake and scared, but that story was nothing to the stuff on TV. It didn't matter, anyway, because Mrs. Fox didn't hear a word Mr. Nagel said. And when everybody started to clap for her to tell the other one, she did.

The fire threw moving shadows across us and smelled of the woods. Mrs. Fox hunched up her shoulders and began slowly in a deep, dark voice. "It was," she began quietly, "a deep, dark, stormy night . . . in a deep, dark, enchanted forest." She waited for the rumble of faraway thunder to stop. "And in that deep, dark, haunted graveyard. And in that deep, dark, yawing hole. And in that deep, dark, yawing hole . . ." Her voice got lower and quieter and quivered a little. ". . . there was a deep . . . dark . . . moldy . . . box." She stopped and said nothing for about fifteen seconds. "And in that deep . . . dark . . . moldy box . . ."

She reached into the pocket of her sweater.

". . . there was a *monkey's paw*!" She waved a furry claw like thing at us, and everybody screamed.

When she rubbed Marshall's cheek with the paw, I saw what it was. It was Nicky's hairy hand, shimmering like real in the flicker of the light.

6

HONK

Nicky was mad.

"She stole it," she said, back in the room, cradling the creepy paw in her hands. "She stole it when she got my flashlight. And now I can't use it to scare anybody because everybody knows."

"It's an awful hand, even when you know," I said, watching her wobble it. "Maybe you could try making three wishes."

She tossed it to me. "You try," she said.

I wish I was home, I thought automatically, since we'd left. The paw moved in my hand.

I swear. "I take that back," I said out loud, and threw the paw to Emily.

"I wish the lights would go on," she said.

Three flashlights, like torches, lit our room.

Ruby's batteries had burnt out, so hers was back in the suitcase. Because we couldn't go running up to kids flapping the old hand at them, we threw pillows at each other instead and moved our beds closer together so we could lie across like bridges.

There was a pay phone in the front hall where Miss Glass had stood to give us apples, I didn't have any money, but I remembered what my dad told me once about calling collect if I was desperate.

I was desperate. I wasn't going to be able to sleep if I couldn't call home. So I headed, with my flashlight off, straight into the dark.

"Going to the job," I announced as I left.

Ruby said to wait up, but I moved as quickly as I could with one hand on the wall. I decided it was safer to travel with my flashlight off. If they couldn't find me, they couldn't find, they couldn't stop me. I edged along toward where I thought the phone was, shuffling slowly, my bare feet cold on the boards. I ran flat into a wall where I didn't think there was one, so I flicked on my flash until I spotted the phone. Nobody arrested me.

Kids were still yelling in their rooms, and I could see beams of light dancing around the boys's stairs as they passed by the top.

I stood quietly, listening for footsteps and watching for lights. I'd never made a call like this, and for all I knew it couldn't really be done for free. So I picked up the receiver, turned my light on the dial, and pushed the 0 for Operator. I told him what I wanted to do, but, since it was a long distance call, he gave me a lot of numbers and when I started to push them I couldn't remember the right order. I hung up. What if I called Moscow by mistake?

I punched 0 again. A man answered this time and I tried harder to remember. Aiming my light on the numbers, I pushed 1-312-212-2786. Somebody, not my mother, answered. "May I help you?" I explained I wanted to call home and have my parents pay and she said, "Your name?" And I told her, Kim Street, their daughter.

The phone at the other end rang and rang and rang and rang. Fifteen times I counted, but nobody answered. My parents were always tired after work. They never went places on Monday nights. It must have been time for the ten O'clock news. They were out looking for the cat. They were closing the guy who stole my bike. No, they had both moved away forever.

I didn't hang up the phone. I just let the receiving swing loose, ringing. My eyes were stinging. I felt like a baby.

Nicky and Ruby are going to wonder if I've fallen in, I thought, and I started to feel my way back to the room, the phone buzzing behind me. As I slid my hand along the wall, I suddenly got this incredibly eerie feeling all the way down to my toes.

Someone else's hand was on top of mine, sliding.

We both gasped.

"Who are you?" a voice whispered. And that's when Emily's wish was granted. All of the lights, all over the place, went on. It was so bright it hurt your eyes like the sun.

Mr. Ivanovitch looked at are like I'd just stepped off a UFO. "What are you doing here, Kim?" He was wearing a bathrobe of the fuzzy brown stuff they make teddy bears out of.

I swallowed hard. "Taking a walk," I said.

"How about you?"

"Me, too." He stared at me for a minute, frowned, and then reached out and wiped a tear off my cheek. I pushed his hand away, so he stuck both of them in his pockets. One of them came right back out with some coins in it.

"Actually, I'm going to use the telephone," he said. "It's not against the rules for adults."

The phone was still ringing, and we both could hear it.

"I tried my folks but nobody was there."

"Homesick?" he asked, gently.

"I forgot something." Trying to explain, I said, "The cat ran away. Also, I think my folks are getting a divorce." I shrugged. "Nobody answers. I guess they've both left." And no matter how hard I tried, I couldn't keep my eyes dry. "I want to go home," I told him.

He bit his lip and looked at me for a while. "Kim, I wish I could just tell you everything's OK, but I don't know if it is," he said. "But, whatever, it'll wait until Wednesday. It's waited this long." He walked over to a grocery sack on the floor and brought out a big bag of marshmallows.

"We were going to roast these tonight in the fire," he said, "but we figured it wouldn't be safe with all those sticks in the pitch dark."

"Potentially dangerous," I said, with a little laugh, remembering the *Guinness Book of World Records*. I popped a marshmallow into my mouth and chewed. The sweet, soft goo of it was wonderful. He probably wouldn't understand if I pretended it was poisoning me.

"Why, Kim, I had no idea you had such an impressive vocabulary. Your parents must be very proud of you."

"I do want to go home," I told him. 'Please, isn't there some way?"

"Not unless you could get Mrs. Fox to drive you, and then you'd have to have a pretty good reason."

"I don't want to talk to Mrs. Fox about it."

"Then you're going to have to hang in there."

On the floor near the phone the snack box had an apple left in it from the afternoon. I reached over, grabbed it, and fled back to the room.

All the kids who'd tried to go to bed earlier when the lights were out were up now, wandering the rooms like it was morning.

"What took you?" Ruby asked. "I had to borrow Nicky's flashlight.

"I was staring, so I stole an apple," I told her, stuffing into my mouth whole, like I was a roast pig.

Nicky was pressing something against the ceiling light.

"It's a glow-in-the-dark Frisbee," she said. "My flashlight wouldn't charge it enough."

Emily wasn't there.

"She went whispering off to Miss Planet," Ruby said. "What on baby."

"Really?" I asked, wondering if my eyes looked all red and my cheeks striped.

Miss Planet, Mrs. Fox, and Miss Glass were all calling, "Lights out."

"Again?" I yelled. "We're just getting used to them.

Emily hurried back in, staring at her feet, I couldn't look for tear streaks.

"Did she give you your baby bottle?" Ruby asked.

"No," Emily said, breathing funny. "She gave me my pills."

"You do drugs?" Nicky asked, giggling.

"They're for asthma," Emily explained, climbing into bed. "I can't help it."

Miss Planet strolled in, plucked the apple core from my hand, and said, "The creatures of the night might smell this delicacy and decide to attack. I'll drop it in the garbage for you." Then she turned to Emily. "How're you doing, friend.

"Fine," Emily said, rasping. As she turned in bed, I could see that under the camp trotter blanket there was another one. It was blue with bunnies.

She *is* a baby, I thought. Ruby's right.

That kid really *is* a baby. Baby Emily, I said to myself. I've got stuff to worry about, and that's why I'm feeling so bad. But this kid is a total loss.

Miss Planet pressed the switch and it was dark again, but not too dark. The hall lights stayed on and we could see in the din. We threw the glow-in-the-dark Frisbee back and forth between Nicky and me and Ruby. Emily even flung it a couple of times when we let her. But then Mrs. Fox barged in and took it away.

"Girls, girls, girls, it's bedtime, bedtime," she boomed, more like a cannon than a lullaby.

And baby Emily probably needs a lullaby, I thought, laughing to myself.

In the desk we talked about lots of stuff. About the storm, about the monkey's paw, about Miss Planet and Mr. Ivanovitch getting married. Emily and Ruby were surprised, but they liked the idea. Emily was even laughing about how Sam Fox was silly, thinking Miss Planet would *ever* marry him. That's when we heard the strange noise, a kind of buzzing near the floor. I struck my head over the side and saw Ruby, lying on her back with her mouth open, really chuffing out the snores. It's a wonder she wasn't walking herself up. We took turns shouting at her, thinking that would put a stop to it, but she snored on, turning over on her side and pulling her knees up to her chest.

Emily took a flashlight from under her bed and turned it on Ruby's bunch. Ruby never had tucked her sheets and blanket in. It looked like she was sleeping in a clothes dryer.

"She's out," Emily said. "Boy, I wish I could get to sleep that fast."

"You're lucky you didn't tonight," Nicky told her, flicking her flashlight on. "I decided that tonight we'd truck the first guy who went to sleep."

"Truck? What's truck?" Emily asked, laughing nervously.

"You haven't been to camp, have you?" Nicky said.

I didn't know what trucking was either, but I didn't say so.

"What you do is this," Nicky explained. "Emily, you grab your pillow." Emily grabbed.

The top of her baby blanket hung over the edge of her bed.

"Kim and I'll get our flashlights out and what we do is this: Emily, you hit Ruby over the head with your pillow. Kim and I will stand about two feet apart and we'll shine our flashlights at Ruby and then we'll all yell, Truck! Truck! Watch out for the truck! So when she wakes up she'll think our flashlights are headlights coming straight at her."

"And she'll have a heart attack," Emily laughed.

"Somebody did it to me last summer." Nicky said, and I'm still alive.

"Did it scare you?" I asked.

"Yeah," she said, "spit less."

Somebody was walking down the hall in shoes, which meant it was an adult type, still dressed and checking. We lay still for a few minutes until there were no more hall sounds. There was only Ruby, ripping the air with her snores.

"She deserves it, you know, for keeping us awake," Emily said, climbing out of bed with her pillow.

I got my flashlight, Nicky got hers, and we started on tiptoe, shoulder to shoulder, flashlight even, walking straight from the door toward Ruby.

We were a huge semi tooling down the highway at ninety miles an hour.

"Now!" Nicky called.

"Honk!" Emily shouted, pounding Ruby with her pillow, really smashing her one.

"Truck!" Nicky yelled, and we drove straight at Ruby.

"Truck! It's coming straight at you," I shouted.

"Truck!"

Ruby stopped snoring, sat up in bed, and stuck her arms out like she was trying to stop whatever was going to crash into her. Ducking, she rolled out of bed and onto the floor.

We laughed like crazy, Emily most of all.

Miss Planet stuck her head in the doorway.

"I've had just about enough of this foolishness. We can hear you clear it at the other end of the hall.

"Sorry," we all mumbled, all but Ruby.

Ruby was foaming.

"You hit me," she told Emily when Miss Planet had left. "I felt you hit me."

"It was just a pillow," Emily said, crawling back into bed, still laughing. "It couldn't have hurt."

Ruby stood up and walked over to Emily.

"Don't you dare laugh at me, Emily. Don't you dare." She didn't say it loud enough for Miss Planet to hear, just low and mean. "You may have scared me out of my sleep, but at least I don't go around scared *all* the time, afraid to leave my mommy and my daddy. And I didn't need a huggy-poo from Mr. Nagel when the mean, bad, old lightning flashed. And," she said, leaning over and giving a sharp yank, "I didn't have to bring a baby blanket from home to suck my thumb with." She waved the blanket over her head to make Emily reach up for it.

"It helps me sleep," Emily said softly.

"Ruby didn't seem mad at Nicky and me, even though we were the truck that almost smashed her.

"I think I'm going to sue you," she said to Emily. "Like at school. Only I'll sue you for waking me up."

"I wasn't the only one."

"Maybe, but you hit me and I didn't do anything to you. You're just the baby who wants her baby blanket." She threw the blanket to me and I held it. It was soft and smelled sour.

"You admitted you did it, so you're guilty."

Ruby went on. "And you aren't even sorry, because you were laughing."

"The one who sues you can't be the judge," Emily told her. And we know from school that was true.

"In this court she can," Ruby said.

"It was a joke," I explained to Ruby. "It's something called trucking. You were supposed to be scared silly, that's all."

"It wasn't funny. She hurt my head." She turned back to Emily in her bunk. "You are guilty and I fine you . . ."

"I didn't bring any money with me," Emily said, eyeing her blanket and breathing again with a wheeze. "They said not to."

"OK. No money. Nicky, got any ideas for a punishment?" Ruby asked, laughing suddenly, as though this was really just a big joke.

"You got something to scare *her* silly?"

"Sure," Nicky said, laughing with her.

I think we were both glad Ruby wasn't going to lash out at us too. "Make her go up and steal a teddy bear from the boy's floor and sleep with that tonight instead of her blanket."

I didn't say anything. I guess I could have, but I didn't.

Ruby put on her official judge's voice and said, "I find you, Emily, guilty of waking me up by hitting me when I hadn't done anything to you. Your punishment is to go get some dumb toy from the boys' floor."

Emily started to say something, but Ruby went on. "If you don't we'll take your baby blue blanket to breakfast tomorrow and pass it around to show everybody the bunnies."

"Give it to me," Emily begged.

"When you come back," I told her. "After you've done it, you won't be afraid anymore."

Maybe she believed me, because she crawled out of her bed and left the room.

"I bet," Nicky said, "She's on her way to tell Miss Planet on us."

"You think so?" Ruby asked! "That would be a rotten thing to do."

We walked to the door quietly, all three of us, and looked down the lighted hall, but Emily wasn't anywhere. In the room next to ours we could hear Mrs. Fox rumble like small thunder.

"She's *snoring*!" Ruby whispered, giggling.

"How gross!"

Nicky and I looked at each other and laughed. Ruby didn't even know she'd been snoring.

"I tell you what. Let's *truck* her!" Ruby whispered, and we all laughed without making a noise.

We went back into the room though, and waited.

"Maybe she ran away or something," I said after a few minutes. "Maybe we were too mean."

"Mean? What'd you mean, *mean*?" Ruby laughed.

"You're the one who told her it'd be good for her. We're just building her character, right?"

I picked the blue blanket off my back and folded it over Emily's pillow. Then I climbed up and sat cross-legged on my bed.

When she finally ran in, Emily was heaving like she'd been swimming a mile. She hadn't been telling on us or running away, though. In her hand was a gray stuffed kitten with a red bow around its neck. She flung it at Ruby.

"Here," she said. "You *sleep* with it."

Climbing into bed, she turned her head to the wall. I looked over the edge of my bed, but I couldn't tell if she was crying or just mad. Nobody was laughing.

I got up and went to the bathroom, because I'd forgotten to before when I tried to call home. As I was washing my hands, I looked up and saw a printed sign I hadn't noticed there before. It said "The Most Dangerous Animal in the World." The sign was over a mirror. And in the mirror was me.

7

CROCS IN THE GRASS, ALAS

"SYRUP! Hopper, more maple syrup!" R.X demanded, like she was master and I was slave. She stuffed half a slice of bread into her month and passed the pitcher back. Sure enough, it was empty. French toast floated in pools of syrup on plates all around the table, but at least two kids hadn't got it yet.

"People, you are wasting food. I don't like it one bit," Mr. Nagel said sternly. "And I want to see you cutting your food into smaller pieces." R.X looked up at the ceiling. Would she let me dip my French fries in catsup if I went to that lunch I'd won? Fat chance. Maybe I could wiggle out my back tooth just at noon on Thursday, and suffer too much to go.

Everybody was quiet, looking down at our French toast islands. But the pitcher did have a spoonful left in it, so I tilted my white chef's cap on my head and went to the kitchen for more.

After breakfast was over and I'd scraped all the sticky plates and taken the last sweep with the sponge, I went outside with Sam, who'd been hopper at the next table. It was sunny, and so warm we didn't even need jackets. We inspected an oak tree next to the front steps. It had a white slit down the side where lightning had torn the bark away.

"Who won your scavenger hunt last night?"

Sam asked as we hurried back to the lodge. Inspection was in fifteen minutes and I hadn't made my bed. "Scavenger hunt?" I asked.

"You know," Sam said impatiently, "the one I gave Emily my grey cat for. Who won it?"

"Oh, that scavenger hunt," Emily, you fox, I thought, that wasn't bad at all. I'd wondered why a posse hadn't come cat hunting. "Emily won," I told him. "She won because of your cat, but Ruby slept with it, so you'll have to get it back from her."

"You're kidding!" he said. Then he shrugged his shoulders. "I don't care if Ruby likes me or not. She's not cueshee. We thought the rest of you would be coming, you know, looking for more cats. And we waited for you. Actually," he said as we got to the lodge, "we were waiting on both sides of our door with pillows ready to smash you over the head. But we laughed so much that when we whammed our four pillows at the first guy who walked through the door, it was Mr. Ivanovitch checking on the noise. He got such a blast it probably made him even taller." Sam giggled.

"What'd he do?"

"He said if we weren't quiet, he was going to drag his mattress into our room and camp out on the floor. So we shut up and went to sleep. That would have been pure poison."

Our room did not win inspection. We didn't even come close. Miss Planet stood with her arms crossed while Ruby stuffed her pajamas into a drawer and tucked in her sheets, sort of. And when Miss Planet pulled Sam's red-bowed cat from under Ruby's bunk, nobody claimed it.

Mrs. Fox yodeled, and we gathered on the front porch in our four sections. Mr. I. Explained that what his group was going to do first was called the log jam, which sounded pretty weird.

We followed him up the hill, through the woods, and into a clearing, where there was a genuine log on the ground.

"OK, Tape," he said. "All aboard." It wasn't a very thick log—only about a foot across—though it was so long it could have at least twenty kids. We climbed on it and stood there like thirteen bumps.

"One thing about being human," Mr. Ivanovitch said, "is that you can think. It isn't just instinct that makes us tick. This is a kind of puzzle to see if you can get yourself out of a mess by using your heads." The thirteen of us teetered on the log.

"The mess you're in now," he explained, "is that on all sides of that log you're on there in quick sand, and if you step off the log, the quick sand will suck you under. Got that?"

I looked down at the solid ground and imagined it was something oozy, like oatmeal.

"This is creepy," Lewis said.

"So, here is the puzzle." He pointed with a stick to a place between Emily and Sam roughly in the middle of the log. "The six of you on one side of this middle line have to exchange places with the seven on the other side without falling off into the wire."

We stood there for a minute, rocking.

"Is this a trick question?" Sam asked.

"If we were grasshoppers, no problem," Michelle said.

"It's not possible."

"How do we do it?" Mr. Ivanovitch said.

People started talking all at once, with nobody listening. And no matter what we tried, we fell off. If that quicksand would have been little oozier we'd all have been sucked into the centre of the earth. "Let's do something fun," Cyrus from 4A moaned.

"It can't be done," I said.

"Of course it can. But you're going to have to help each other, instead of fighting. You may even have to touch each other," Mr. Ivanovitch explained.

"Me, touch him?" Nicky said, poking Cyrus in the ribs. He jumped to the front, yelled,

"Cookies!" and poked her back. She fell into the quicksand. It was useless.

"I know!" Lewis said. "I've got an idea. One half kind of squat down, like . . ."

"I've got a better idea," Sam yelled. "All we've got to do..."

"But if we . . ."

"Listen to Lewis," Michelle said.

"Then *say* it," Sam told him impatiently.

"OK," Lewis began for the millionth time, "my team, spread out so there's like, a foot or so between each person. And then squat down very low. The other team can just step over us . . . sort of like leapfrog."

"Then we'll have changed sides. He's right, you know," Michelle said.

A few of us fell off anyway, but it worked better than anything else we'd tried.

So we collapsed on the ground that was no longer quicksand.

"Was it the right answer?" Lewis asked.

"It worked," Mr. Ivanovitch told him. "Congratulations, Lewis," and Lewis beamed.

"That was easy," Sam said. "Let's do something else."

We did a whole batch of people puzzles. In one we had to crawl through triangles of rope that were supposed to be electric fences. We ran through a maze of Irises and climbed over a slippery log that was lashed about six feet off the ground between two trees. That wasn't any piece of cake. I was dangling with my head and arms over the log, desperate for help, when Nicky yelled up,

"It's OK, Kim. If you fall, I've got this great little graveyard for you." Michelle who was sitting up on the log, grabbed me by the belt and pulled me over safe.

The last puzzle we did was using two plants to get all of us across five tree stumps. Sam kept trying to boss us, but his ideas didn't always work. So, when Arthur said, "We've got to cooperate, you guys," Sam asked him if *Sesame Street* was his very *very* favorite show. Arthur was right, though. It never worked when we were arguing.

"Watch out!" Mr. Ivanovitch yelled whenever we stumbled. "There are crocs in the grass, alas!" By the time we were through, we'd each have at least one toe bitten off by the crocodiles who were supposed to be starving underneath the tree stumps. We were tired, too.

"You're clever," Mr. Ivanovitch said. "No doubt about that. I'll keep that in mind. Now, if you can make it with all your wounds, we're going to capture some small creatures and have a race." And he started off in the direction of the lodge.

"We may be smart," I said to the Tapes I was walking with, "but there's something in the girls dorm . . ." Everybody laughed. "No, really. There's this sign in there above the mirror."

"There's a sign in the boys' bathroom, too," Lewis told me. "The Most Dangerous Animal in the World."

"What's so dangerous about me?" I asked, though I was afraid I knew. "I mean, the animals out here are always eating each other up."

"Don't be silly. That's a joke mirror," Sam said.

"No, it's not," Emily told him.

Mr. Ivanovitch told us to hunt animals on the way back and put them in little screened boxes he'd brought along. As we searched Mr. Ivanovitch called, "Don't hurt them, my dears. When we're finished we'll free them so they can tend to their business." I thought about my picture in the mirror and didn't catch anything.

"It's like a scavenger hunt, don't you think, Emily?" I said.

Her eyes turned suspicious. "Who told you?"

The two of us shook a bush and woke a bee, which we did not follow.

"Sam," I said, smiling brightly. "And I think that was very very very clever. I wouldn't have thought of it myself."

She did not smile back.

Nobody caught a fox and put it in a box, or an armadillo or a camel, either. We did a cricket, a centipede, a big black ant, and even, down by the marsh, a small frog.

Arthur soaked his sneakers bugging him.

We took our animals to an open spot, drew a big circle in the dirt, put them in the middle, and watched to see which would get out of the circle first. I thought it would be the frog easy, because it was the biggest.

So did most people. But it wasn't. The frog just sat there.

"He's scared stiff," Nicky said.

The cricket jumped back and forth, getting nowhere.

"He's scared silly," Emily laughed, and the three of us from room nine smiled at each other.

The centipede ambled along. But the big black ant made it out in less than a minute. He didn't even wait for his Trophy.

8

DOWN ON THE FARM

"Come on, it won't hurt you. Who'll hold it? How about you, little boy?" Lunch was over. We'd finished planning skits for the night's fireside program, and we Tapes were back to nature again, learning about bird banding.

Sam backed off. Either he didn't want to be called "little boy" or he was afraid to hold a pecky little yellow warbler.

The camp Trotter guide had just taken the warbler out of a metal mesh cage that had seeds in it. Sometime during the morning the dumb bird had just hopped right in and gotten caught. The camp Trotter man meant to snap a metal band around its leg, giving the bird a number for identification, but the bird already had a band. "This is one of last year's," he said, and he handed the bird to me without asking if I wanted it.

Everybody stared as I took it. There was no way to say no. He started talking about migration and stuff, but I couldn't follow what he said because I had this wild bird cupped in my hands.

It pecked at my thumbs like needle pricks when you're getting a splinter out. Its claws scratched at my little fingers, and its heartbeat as fast as a purr against my palms. My heart beat fast, too. He wanted to go home. So did I

"Can I let him go?" I asked, interrupting.

"Anybody else want a turn?" He looked around. Nobody else did.

"Hold fast," Mr. Ivanovitch called. "I remembered my camera this afternoon." He took a picture of me and the bird, neither one of us looking happy. And then I let it fly away home.

After the bird banding place, we hiked to the farm. Mr. Ivanovitch lined us up in pictures all together. Then he snapped kids sitting in the old claw-foot bathtub filled with hay in the farmyard. Kids grabbed hay and stuck it in the other kids' shirts and into their hair, great fistfuls of it, wanting pictures of that, too.

"Don't play with their food," he called. And he snapped the lens cap back on the camera.

A baby goat wandered up and nuzzled his leg. "Oh, look, do," he said, "it's the new kid in town."

"Mr. Ivanovitch, that's terrible." Arthur told him giggling. The little kid sprang forward, Ka-pong, Ka-pong, and two bigger goats chased after it. So did Vinny from 4A.

Inside the barn, chickens sat on nests.

I'd never seen a chicken on a nest before.

"Are there any eggs?" Mr. Ivanovitch asked.

"I don't see any," Michelle told him, holding her hands behind her back as she looked.

"Reach under the hens and check."

"You're kidding," Sam said, taking a step away. The hens' heads shifted toward him.

"They'll attack."

Emily marched right up to the nest, struck her hand under the hen, and brought out an egg. "Like magic," she said, holding it up with two fingers.

"Why is it brown?" Lewis asked. "That's like gross."

"Because it's a brown egg," she told him.

"Real eggs are white," he said. Like, I never saw a brown egg before, and I've been eating eggs all my life. The eggs in the grocery store are white." He looked at it closely, his nose wrinkled. "Is it safe to eat?" he asked Mr. Ivanovitch.

"Some are just brown and some are white. It depends on the chicken," Emily went on. "Chicken eggs are chicken eggs. My grandparents have a farm, and that's how I know." She reached under another hen and brought out one more brown egg. If Emily could do that without flinching, why did she need a baby blanket? It didn't make sense.

A black-and-white cat tunneled from under the barn. Vinny and I both chased it, but I swooped it up. "I found an owl," I called to Nicky, and everybody else thought I was bonkers. It was the same hard-purring cat I'd carried to the lodge the day before.

From the farm we could see the cemetery, only a city block or so away. But we didn't have paper with us. Besides, there was no way to sneak over. Mr. Ivanovitch was thinking about the cemetery, too.

"I wonder if I could break away for a couple of minutes and make a fast rubbing," he said, almost to himself. He fingered a roll of paper in the big bag he carried over his shoulders, chewed on his lip, and then looked at his watch. He signed and said, "It's three o'clock, my dears, and we're supposed to be in those orange pontoon boats ready to measure the depth of lovely Lake Lindalomas at three-ten.

A goat who wanted its picture taken before we left began to nibble on his camera.

"OK, put the rabbits back in their hutches. We've got to leave."

"This rabbit is totally like velvet," Arthur told him. "Pet it."

Vinny, chasing after a rabbit she'd put down to see if it would hop, slipped in a slick of mud and fell flat.

"Oh, my dear, you look as though you could grow a crop of corn on those jeans along," Mr. Ivanovitch said as he scraped her off with a stick and splashed her with water from the pump.

Sam struck a brown egg under the flow of water. "Can I take this back with me?" he asked.

"I hesitate to ask what you'd *do* with an egg. Sam, but the answer, in any case, is no. It belongs on the farm. It may even have had plans to be a baby chick."

Finally he checked to see that everything was in place, locked up, and then announced, "In the boats! We're going to take the temperature of the lake and test it for bacteria. So, if you fall in, we'll know how deep you'll sink, how cold you'll be, and what's alive in there with you."

We looked like scarecrows, hay stacking out of our pockets and shirts. And as we marched, Mr. Ivanovitch told us that we were off to see the blizzard of the Docks, who was going to tell us all about Alice in Wonderland.

"See," Arthur whispered to Sam. "He's even funny like Miss Planet when you give him a chance."

Sam rolled his eyes. "A laugh riot," he said.

By supper time we were tired and hungry. Even kids who didn't like meatloaf loaded it with catsup and ate. Though they had been quiet most of the day, my woollyworms had an appetite too. Besides, meatloaf is one of my favorites.

After supper, Nicky conned two sheets of drawing paper and a couple of crayons out of Mr. Stafford, telling him we had this art project we needed to work on. But by the time we'd played another kickball game and seen a film on bats in the recreation room, I was zonked out. I was ready to draw a lake, a couple of trees, and a cat, give that to Mr. Ivanovitch, and call it quits.

"The fire is going strong," Mr. Ivanovitch called when the movie was over, and I looked out of the window, half expecting to see smokey the Bear shaking his finger at him.

"Oh, my, a campfire, that's glorious," Mrs. Fox announced, pulling herself up from the flowered sofa. "Shall I tell another fireside story? I have a treasury of them."

"Not tonight," Mr. Nagel said, a little too fast and little too loud. "Last night was charming," he added, "and we thank you very much, of course, but tonight we have Silence, Skits, and Singing."

9

HERE, KITTY, KITTY

Silence came first. Except for some tripping and burping, we walked in total, mysterious quiet through the woods and up a hill into a clearing. The fire wasn't there. They had us all lie down in a circle, our feet towards the middle, so we could stare up at the millions of stars. The moon looked like a canoe.

First we searched for star pictures, but I never do see bears up there or Hercules or the three parts of anybody's belt. The Big Dipper, that's easy. But that's all.

Then they told us to lie still with our eyes closed and listen to the sounds of the night. It's told that with your eyes closed you hear better. Somehow, you'd think that so far from the city and shopping centers and cars and all it would be quiet, but it wasn't. *We* were quiet for once, but the crickets rubbed their legs nonstop, and the trees made a racket when the wind blew through them. Chains clinked where the boats were tied down at the pier, a plane flew over, and a dog barked far away

After we'd listened to night noises for a while, Miss Planet said she was going to call an owl and see if one could answer. Lying on the ground with us, one of the spokes of our wheel, she told us how owls are predators and what they eat. Big owls sometimes catch skunks, she said. Owls don't even care if they get sprayed with the stink, because they've got a lousy sense of smell. Small owls swallow mice and birds and snails whole, she said, and after they eat, they spit out pellets of all the leftover fur and bones and feathers. Everybody went "Yuck." She waited a little and then went "Woo-woo," kind of soft like a pigeon.

Nothing answered, except the leaves and the crickets and the clinking chains.

"Wooooo," she went again.

I shivered. What if this huge owl swooped down, picked up the smallest kid in the ring—Trace probably—laid his pellet on us and flew away without a noise? Miss Planet had said their wings were soundless.

"Woooo-oooo," Miss Planet tried again. She was just two down from me and I knew it was still her calling, but I heard kids say, "I heard one answer, did you?"

Miss Planet *woo*-ed once more, and after a while cleared her throat and said, "Some owls hoot, some laugh, some shriek." I think she was giving us a lecture to make up for the bird's not answering her. "Some owls snoring," she went on. That broke everybody up. Owls snoring. The only owl that was going to answer us was a laughing owl.

"I know how to call birds," Nicky said, turning her head to me.

"Sure. Sure you do," I told her.

"I *do*. It's easy." She raised her voice. "Here, bird! Here, bird!" And from somewhere near in the woods, a bird answered, "Wooooo-Wooooo."

We couldn't stay flat any longer. Everybody was eyes open and whistling like you do for a dog and calling. "Here, birdie! Here, owl!" and the silence was gone for good.

Next came singing. We walked to the camp fire mumbling this song we'd learned in music class before we left school. It was about "jolly flames a dancing" and "pale moonlight entrancing."

Mr. Ivanovitch had been in charge of making the fire and it was a knockout, shaped like a teepee and spitting sparks up like crazy.

Sitting logs were set in a big ring around the fire. Kids kept shifting around on them until they got Miss Planet and Mr. Ivanovitch, next to each other, because by then everybody knew for sure they were practically engaged.

The fire felt warm on our faces, and we were all sitting there smelling the wood burn. When Miss Glass stood up and raised her hand, we were already almost quiet. Miss Glass was in charge of the program she called Fireside Fun.

"First, we're going to play a warm-up game," she announced, "called Telephone. What I'll do is whisper a sentence to the two people on each side of me and we'll hear how it changes. That way you can see how well you're learned to listen." A few people groaned. But since she was just a student teacher, Miss Glass might not have known.

She started out the same thing going opposite directions around the circle and after it had gotten whispered one way through twenty ears, it came out, "A glove ate more thread than my damp daughter." Miss Glass said that wasn't right. At the other end, Vinny said was "I shove trout ashore dead and they're hotter." Miss Glass hadn't started with that either, it turned out. She'd said, "I love outdoor Ed at Camp Trotter." It was better our way.

Then it was a skit time. Each group had worked one out. The Lindalomas all got up and sang "Great Green Gobs of Greany Grimy Gopher Guts." The Bowls did a skit about a barber shop I never did understand, but it had a lot of screaming and catsup in it. The CIA wound kids up in rolls of toilet paper they called Do-It-Yourself-Mummy bits.

The Scotch Tape did Fortune Teller. It was Sam's idea, so he got to be Swami. He sat cross-legged, a towel draping his head and a sheet twined around him like a cape. He faced the campfire and swayed back and forth, asking the spirit of the Great outdoors to help him read fortunes.

He read fortunes from shoes. Each of the rest of the tape brought him a shoe to read. He turned the first one over carefully, stared at its bottom, and said in his high, flutey voice, "You have a beautiful soul." Kids groaned, but he went on, "And you will go on TV or be in other fancy shoe business." The groans got louder. The shoe belonged to R.X, who tap dances. Sam flicked it over his shoulder, and R.X ran to pick it up before somebody else could.

Over a pair of somebody's high-toppers he shrieked, "You're so high-strung!" Then he tossed that shoe behind him, crying, "Let yourself go!"

I brought him one of Marshall's Adidas that had tears along both sides where mud had leaked in. He held his nose with one hand and threw the shoe far away with the other, saying, "You don't give a hoot. You pollute!" Marshall jumped up high to catch the shoe, because Sam had tossed it as far as it was stinky. Somebody else caught it and, Marshall chased after, the shoe got flung from kid to kid like it was a long dead toad.

Then Lewis brought one of Mr. Ivanovitch's heavy, worn hiking boots up. He bowed as he presented it. The corners of Sam's mouth twitched. He closed his eyes, held the boot up high over his head in both hands, and said," This belongs to someone who is going on a long, long trip." He grabbed it by the laces, swung it around in circles, and let it fly. The trip, I guess, was supposed to be to the moon. And, while it didn't orbit, nobody saw where it fell short.

"Next," Sam demanded, holding his hands in front of him like he was in a game.

"Molly," Mr. Nagel said, sharply. "You have thrown the shoe into the bushes. It belongs to Mr. Ivanovitch. We must find it at once."

Sam shook his head like he was trying to wake up. "Oh, my," he said, "I'm so sorry, didn't do it on purpose. Which way did it go?"

Kids started getting up and moving out in all directions. Nobody was sure which way it had gone.

"I'm afraid it's too dark to look now," Mr. Ivanovitch said, "Tomorrow morning will do. It's all right, Sam. You were just too involved in the skit. I expect you'd be a terrific actor!"

Sam smiled. That's what he thought too.

Miss Glass got everybody standing, even thought our skit wasn't really over, and we stood there with a lot more sneakers in our hands. "OK, now, everybody, we'll sing 'Day is Done,'" she said, "because it is." She sounded glad. "Everybody hold hands to sing." Nobody did. "OK, now, everybody hold hands so we can be one big circle, one group, one family." We held, but there was a lot of grumbling, sighing, and coolie-shouting. As we stood, we watched to see if Miss Planet would hold Mr. Ivanovitch's hand, too. She did. It was like happily ever after.

Mr. Ivanovitch was standing on one foot, and after we finished singing "safely rest" at the end, Miss Planet helped him down the path. Nicky winked at me.

On the way back, Nicky and I talked about the night and whether we should go out in it. The moon wasn't even half there, but our own flashlights were still bright.

"Listen," Nicky whispered, "we hit the sack right away and pretend to be asleep. Then we sneak out as soon as Miss Planet has made her bed check."

I yawned and stretched.

"You want to chicken out?" she asked.

I wanted to.

"Listen, you tore that rubbing as much as I did," she said. And that was a fact.

"You guys," Ruby whispered as we walked in the room, "Let's stay up really late and raid somebody." She had plans, too. "Maybe we could cruise around and do a little trucking."

Emily was already in bed. "If you truck me tonight," she told us, "I will let the air out of your tyres and make you crash." She flashed her light in all three of our eyes. It wasn't fair. Emily didn't look homesick anymore. But the night still grabbed at my throat, making it hard for me to swallow. I needed at least to call home and check, but I couldn't let Nicky see me doing it.

We both yawned big and took our shoes off.

I grabbed one of Nicky's and yelled in a high voice, "Oh, your tongue looks furry. It's probably fatal."

Nicky crossed her eyes and collapsed on the floor.

When Ruby left the room, we crawled into bed with our clothes on and turned to the wall so she wouldn't see if our eyes flickered. Then we waited.

Down the hall I could hear kids calling, "I am not!" "Give that back!" "My nose is bleeding."

After lights out, Nicky started to fake snoring, and if I hadn't known what she was doing, I'd have thrown a pillow at her. Ruby complained to Emily about how we weren't having any fun at all, but soon she was snoring, too, for real. I lay there close to the ceiling listening to the crickets outside, wishing it was tomorrow and the bus had just pulled in at school and both my folks were there meeting me with a batch of chocolate chip cookies and telling me how great it was to be the three of us again. And telling me, too, how the fire men had rescued Fido from the top of a TV antenna and how the FBI had found my bike painted gold in a raid on an international bike ring, and how . . . I decided when Nicky got to sleep really, I would get up and call home. The crickets chirped on and on.

"But," I was asking this lady dressed in blue, "but aren't you going to . . . But I thought you fought . . ." And the lady was about to say something very, very important to me when suddenly, "Kim," somebody hissed in my ear. "Kim, come on!" A hand was shaking my shoulder.

"Who . . ." I asked. "What . . . time?"

"We fell asleep," Nicky was telling me. "It's eleven thirty-two. My watch says, come on. Carry your shoes till we get outside, and don't forget your flashlight. I've got the paper and crayon. We ought to be able to do it in an hour."

Rubbing my eyes and shaking the sleep out, I climbed down from the bunk as quietly as I could. We tiptoed through the dimly lighted hall past Mrs. Bosco's room. She was mumbling in her sleep like a cement mixer.

The front door clicked when we opened it, but nobody appeared, so we sat down on the outside steps to put on our sneakers. The crickets weren't asleep yet, but the night was quieter and the air cooler than it had been during Silence and Skits.

All we had to do was follow the road to the graveyard. Looking behind and in front both, we watched for cars and ghosts and teachers. As we jogged, I could feel things alive and watching from both sides of the road, but no one really knew we were there. If we got trucked in the deep, dark night, nobody would know.

By the time we reached the cemetery, I felt like I'd been running a hundred miles, a hundred thousand miles, with some mysterious predator chasing after. Something shaped like a shadow.

Nicky, though, was all excited and she loved it more.

"Don't you feel like you're skipping school and nobody's ever going to find out? This is so excellent," she said as we reached the graveyard.

"I'm tired," I told her, and that's all I could say about how I felt. She'd have rolled on the graves laughing at how I felt. She was scare proof.

As we searched our way down the main path of the cemetery, we heard a car coming on the highway. Flicking our lights off, we fell flat. The dead were quiet in the night. Not even a breeze moved. The car slowed down, but kept going when everything was totally black again, we got up. Nicky turned on her light and located the baby with wings. We took turns rubbing and holding the paper and the light. It was better to be the one rubbing because then you had something to do. I held the paper last, watching for cars and trying not to stare at the tombstones where things seemed to shift in the shadows.

"Can't you hurry?" I asked Nicky. "My fingers are numb."

"Finished!" she said. "One more sweep and I'm finished." She leaned into it.

After the last stroke we sat on the grass away from the wounds and looked at what we'd done.

It was excellent. Except that paper had been moved a very little bit and the angel had a moustache because of it, the rubbing was practically perfect. True, Nicky hadn't checked the color of the crayon and we'd done it in purple instead of black, but it was still excellent. I began to feel good for the first time since she woke me. Rolling the rubbing up into a tube, I looked up at the stars through it and then tucked it under my arm.

On the way back we headed down the middle of the highway like it was the yellow brick road, figuring *everybody* was asleep by twelve-thirteen, the time it said on Nicky's digital watch. We swing our flashlights dark by our sides, though, just in case.

"Hey, Kim, look it's our old friend," Nicky shouted, pointing ahead at the side of the road.

"Here, kitty," she called, running ahead. "Here, owl!" The creature moved toward us slowly as we galloped his way, calling and whistling. And I bet we were only ten feet away before I saw that, while he was black and white, he wasn't our cat. This kitty was big and black and furry with white stripes down the sides and had eyes like tiny read marbles. He was a skunk.

10
SQUIRT

I grabbed Nicky by the arm. "Back up slow or he'll shoot!" I said, my voice squeaking. I pulled at Nicky again, but she didn't move. The skunk eyed us to see, maybe, if we were his friends. I tried a smile but my mouth wouldn't work.

"Hurry," I hissed at Nicky, yanking her arm. But she was like a stone statue. "Please, Nicky." I never knew what it meant before, scared stiff, but that's what Nicky was.

The skunk wasn't scared. He was mad. He stamped his front feet on the pavement and began a low half purr, half growl. Then he lifted his tail high, the white tip hanging limp like a flag no wind. I knew what was going to happen next. I knew because Miss Planet had told us in the class. The skunk was going to turn around, raise that tip, and squirt us straight from jets in his bottom with an oily yellow stink. Everybody had practically rolled on the floor laughing when she told us in school what fantastic backward aim the skunk has.

"Truck!" I gasped in Nicky's ear, thinking that might move her. "Truck!" When it didn't, I grabbed her belt and pulled. Miss Planet had said if the smell got on your clothes, you soaked them in ammonia for a week, buried them in the ground for a week, and then threw them away. She didn't say what you did with the people inside.

The skunk arched his back and hissed again.

Like I was Superman, I dragged Nicky down the road toward the graveyard. But when I couldn't go any farther, I rolled us off into the ditch and grabbed my nose. Nicky sucked in her breath. I think she'd been holding it all the time. "It . . . never . . . knees . . . locked," she gasped.

As we lay hiding, listening to our hearts bump and our breath heave, I realized that the air I was gulping tasted like ditch dirt and nothing worse. Letting go off my nose, I found out it was true. The skunk hadn't sprayed yet.

"Whoooo," I heard, somewhere in the distance. "Whooo." Owls, I remembered, eat skunks. Owl is predator. Skunk is prey.

"Whoooo," I answered low. "Woooooo." The owl, what if that owl hears me, swoops over, snatches the skunk up for a midnight snack, and carries him away in the sky? What if?

"You crazy?" Nicky whispered, no longer speechless. "Now he'll find us sure." We listened and heard nothing. No skunk, no owl. "Maybe he's gone. Can you see?"

Slowly I raised my head out of the ditch and looked. At first everything was fuzzy and dark, then about thirty feet away, maybe, I saw the skunk. And the skunk saw me. I was certain of it. Maybe it *was* the "whooo's" or maybe he just smelled us, but he knew for sure where we were. And he was heading straight at us down our yellow brick road.

I was just sinking back down in a panic when I turned my head to look again. The skunk wasn't alone. I blinked my eyes to see clearer. Coming over the top of the hill behind, a flashlight beam swept the road and the ditch.

"Ki-m! Ni-cky!" a voice called. I couldn't see who had the flashlight, but I knew we'd been found out.

"Kim! Nicky! Where are you?" the voice cried. Steaming down the highway, gaining on our skunk, was Mr. Ivanovitch. When he stopped yelling, I called back. I had to.

"Skunk!" I sang out quietly, hoping he would hear and the skunk couldn't. "Skunk!" He better not understand English, I thought, and think I'm calling him to come. "Skunk!" Please, Mr. Ivanovitch, I wished, closing my eyes tight, please don't rush up to pet the kitty.

I waited as long as I could stand it. Then, lifting my head again, just eye-level over the ditch, I tried to see what was happening.

His flashlight still glowed and the skunk marched on—our way. Nicky lay face down on her arm, breathing hard. Hiding my head again, I looked up at the stars, quadrillions of them, too many to wish on, but I wished anyway. I am asleep and this is some weird dream, I decided. Or a nightmare, maybe, galloping out of control. That girl Dorothy in The Wizard of Oz, all she had to do was say "There's no place like home," and she got there. There's no place like home, I thought as hard as I could, clenching my fists. There's no place like home. But I could hear paws on the pavement now, and the dirt was not my bed.

"He's coming," I barely breathed out aloud. "Freeze."

"Last time, you said run," Nicky sobbed.

The paw steps clicked closer and clear until I could hear breathing, too. It is the year, I thought of the stink. Forever after they are going to remember this Outdoor Ed as the Big Stink. The whole place will reek of us unless they soak us in ammonia or bury us for a week. The footsteps stopped, but the breathing didn't.

At the edge of the ditch, the pointy faced skunk was peering at me. I did not close my eyes. I did not blink them, even I did sweat. He opened his mouth and his teeth shone. He'd won the battle paws down. Maybe he was laughing. For sure he wasn't scared. All he had to do was whip around, lift his tail, and aim *rat-a-tat-tat.*

Instead, though, he stood there for a minute staring, and then, swishing his vast bushy tail, he turned and disappeared down the road.

Even after his footsteps had faded, we waited five minutes—ten—a long time, listening, until all we could hear was each other breathing. Maybe he had walked away and then snuck back into our ditch to surprise us from behind. My eyes were closed, my fingers crossed, and my scalp was prickling as if tiny ants were moving in with all their gear when a voice above us whispered, "You OK?"

He smelled like cologne. Mr. Ivanovitch sat down on the side of the road, his feet in the ditch. That's when Nicky began to cry. Actually, it was a sort of a half cry, half laugh.

"He's gone?" Nicky asked.

"He is gone," he said. "Tail down. Saving his spray for something a little more wild than you two." He smiled. He *didn't* say, for this cute trick I'll see to it in fourth grade forever.

"How did you know where we were?" I asked him.

"Well I heard the word 'skunk' kind of floating through the air, but I didn't actually see it until one of you peered from your hiding place," he told us, "and all at once I saw skunk and prey." He looked down at Nicky and shook his head. "I didn't know what to do. It's a genuine problem, I thought, no crocs in the grass, but a real live skunk on the road. I don't know when I've been scared." He stood up and shook her shoulders like he wanted to get rid of the feeling in them.

"It worked," I told him, "doing nothing worked."

"You guys were fantastic," he said, leaning toward us. "What a disaster if you'd panicked."

"If?" Nicky laughed, embarrassed.

"Come on," he said, "it's late."

"Is everybody looking for us?"

"Nobody but me. I thought I knew where you were and I *knew* it was my fault you were there. Look, I ought not to have lashed out at you yesterday. I'm sorry." He brushed his hair back and rubbed his front teeth with his fingers. "Maybe I'm not ready to be a teacher, do you think, losing my temper like that?"

Nicky and I didn't say anything. No teacher had asked us a question like that.

"And maybe," he said, "I should have reported you gone."

I didn't know teachers thought about making mistakes. It was like they were always right and we were supposed to be wrong.

"Race you back," he said, smiling suddenly and starting off. He had no shoes on. He was wearing red-and-green striped socks, which was why we hadn't heard his walking up.

"How'd you know we were gone?" I asked as we started back, brushing chunks of ditch dirt off our clothes.

"Emily," he said, trotting faster.

"How'd *she* know?" Nicky asked, her voice shaking only a little now.

"Actually, she only had clues. When you left she was awake, and she heard you say something about crayon and paper and how it would take only an hour." He made a little bow as he ran and said. "I used my remarkable Sherlock Holmes handy-dandy deductions and figure out what that meant. It meant the graveyard."

"But we left our room late. It was eleven thirty-two exactly. Why did you come in at all? Were you just checking?" Nicky asked him. It was like a mystery, suddenly, since he was Sherlock Holmes.

"Ah, you weren't the only ones awake," he said sighing. We walked easy now, in the dark. "Just after eleven forty-five Emily invaded the boys hall."

"Emily?" Nicky and I said together.

"Somebody disguised as Emily," Nicky told him. "No way she'd do that again."

"Again? No, it was Emily. She appeared at the top of the steps carrying a gray stuffed cat with a red bow. Somebody had set Sam's clock to go off at eleven forty-five, and it charged as loud as the fire alarm at school. The place went wild. Sam had shut the alarm off by the time Emily came, but all the boys were standing in their pajamas, the poor kid hardly knew what to do."

"What *did* she do?" Nicky asked.

"Well, she threw the cat at Sam like it was a football and fled. I think she really had come to talk to me about your leaving, but the boys didn't give her a chance." He shook his head. "I don't know why she had the gray cat."

Nicky and I looked at each other and laughed.

The lodge was in sight now. All the rooms were dark.

"After that," he went on, lowering his voice, "there was the terrific disturbance around midnight in the girls' hall. Michelle, R.X., and some other girls had pushed their bunks together, built a fort by draping their blankets across the beds, and were telling ghost stories that ended up in pillow fights. They howled, and that woke the girls next door. And the girls next door started pounding on the walls. I was right at the top of the steps, so I came down to be stern. What a night!" He laughed.

"But we weren't making any noise," I said. "We weren't *there*."

"Actually," he said, "I had something to talk with you about, and I thought if all the yelling and pounding had woken you . . . "

"To talk with me?"

He looked over at Nicky, who was flashing her light up at the stars. "It'll keep," he said.

Slowly, slowly we crept up at the lodge steps and in the front door. The halls were so quiet you'd think there'd never been a pillow fight inside a blanket fort, or ghosts, or bumps in the night.

He put his finger to his lips, then waved goodbye with both hands. When Nicky had turned into our room, I started back to ask what he'd wanted to tell me, but he was gone. I'd decided there was only one thing he could need to talk to me about. He must know something from home. I thought about following him to the boys' floor, but if I ran into Sam or Lewis I'd never be able to go back to school again.

"Kim," Nicky hissed down the hall, sticking her head out of the door. I hurried into the room. "They catch us in our clothes like this and they'll ask us questions and we've had it."

Ruby was snoring away. Emily sat up in bed and stared at us, her eyes wide open.

"What time is it?" she asked.

"Twelve forty-five," Nicky told her.

"Then it took more than an hour. I was worried," she said, "about the ghosts at midnight. And I kept thinking about deep, dark holes with hairy green hands in them. That place is creepy enough in the daylight." She leaned forward. "Did . . . did he find you?"

"Yeah," Nicky said climbing into her bunk above Ruby. She tossed a heap of dirty clothes on the floor and got under the covers wearing her underwear.

"Are you mad at me for telling?" Emily asked her. "I knew I shouldn't have." She watched me take off my socks. "Look, I know you guys don't get scared like I do, but *anything* could have happened in the night."

"Anything did," I told her.

She looked puzzled, but shrugged it off. "Did you get a good rubbing for Mr. Ivanovitch? He said he was really mad at himself for yelling at you about killing the first one."

"Yeah," I told her, yawning as I climbed into bed. "We got a really good one. We did it in purple. It's got a . . ." and then the panic hit me, pow, in the stomach. "Nicky?" I called. "Nicky!" But she was breathing heavy.

"She's asleep," Emily said, craning her neck to look. "Her mouth is open."

"Nicky!" I called again, anyway. "Do you have the rubbing?" But she didn't. I knew she didn't. I had carried the rubbing myself. And it was lying scrunched in a ditch somewhere down the cemetery road, ants crawling through its tunnel, waiting for a high-tailed skunk to pass by.

11

THE ANNOUNCEMENT

"Beautifully behaved! That's what I have to say, and you can quote me. Beautifully behaved. I would be a chaperone for those lovely, lovely girls any day." As they walked down to breakfast, Mrs. Fox was shouting to the world around and Mr. Nagel in particular how perfect we were. "Not a peep out of them after their nine-thirty bedtime. Not a peep. And *I* am a very light sleeper."

"Um," Mr. Nagel answered. He must have been down for the midnight wall-banging.

Nicky and I, walking behind them, held our knuckles to our mouths to keep from laughing. We also had our fingers holding our noses to keep from smelling. A breeze whipping in cool weather was also blowing in the strong, sharp smell of skunk. It was even worse than I had remembered. Kitty-kitty must have met somebody he didn't like. Maybe the owl came and picked him up by the scruff of his neck. Mrs. Fox pulled her red cowboy neckerchief up over her nose like a bandit.

"And I've kept my lip buttoned about Mr. Ivanovitch," she told Mr. Nagel even louder. "Even when Sam asked specially,

Mr. Ivanovitch was so gracious to him during that daring skit, didn't you think?"

"Um," Mr. Nagel said again. I got the feeling he wasn't crazy about Mrs. Fox, but was too polite to let her know.

"And when will the announcement be?" Mrs. Fox asked.

"I expect he'll decide that," Mr. Nagel answered as R.X., Ruby, and Michelle ran up to join us. Emily had gone down early to be a hopper. We told them about the announcement.

"I guess the boys are right about their getting married," R.X. said, shaking her head. "But that sure was quick. Mr. Ivanovitch only substituted three or four times around school after he substituted for us."

"Once you meet him you don't forget him, though," Michelle said.

Halfway down the hill, Mr. Ivanovitch was walking alone. "I'll be back in a minute," I said to the guys. "There's something I want to find out."

"Find out if we'll be invited. I want to throw rice," Ruby called after me.

"The sheet of instructions said to bring *two* pairs of shoes," I told him as I ran up. He had only one boot on. The shirt under his painters' overalls was blue with big white dots. Today's socks were yellow-and-white.

"The sheet of instructions was for the kids." He shrugged. "Grown-ups don't need two pairs of hiking boots."

"What did you want to tell me last night?" I asked him.

"Let's talk about it later," he said, looking down and walking faster.

"*Now*, please," I begged. My knees turned to Silly Putty, because I could tell he had something to hide, something he didn't want to say.

"After breakfast?" he asked.

"Now!"

Instead of walking into the mess hall, we turned down the road toward the lake.

"Well," he began, glancing back to see if anybody was following us, "last night when everybody *seemed* settled, around ten o' clock if you can believe that, I went down and made a telephone call to . . . to a friend. When nobody answered, I got to thinking about meeting you at the night before and how homesick you seemed, and I thought maybe it would help . . ." He took a deep breath before going on. ". . . maybe it might help if I brought you a big hello from your folks and good news from home, since you couldn't call yourself, and . . . "

"You're kidding. So you *called* them?"

He put his finger to his mouth to quiet me. There were only a dozen or so kids left to go in to breakfast, so he started talking fast.

"I wanted to help." He wiped his palms on his painters' pants and went on. "I've taken lots of psychology courses in school. I don't know why I thought a marshmallow could be the answer."

"What did they say? Were they home?" I didn't see how marshmallows had anything to do with it.

"I spoke to your mother."

"What did she *say*?"

"Well, everything is all right," he began, putting his hand on my arm, "but it isn't. I just don't want you to worry. It's not what you think."

"It's not what I think. It's what everybody *says*."

"Whatever. Your mother was right by the phone when I called. She said she was thinking about calling you, but was afraid it was too late."

"Too *late*?"

"At night."

I sank down on the cold concrete bench overlooking the lake. The skunk smell was almost gone.

"She was going to tell you," Mr. Ivanovitch said, sitting beside me, "that your father is in the hospital. He had gallstones."

"Hospital? Gallstones? I never heard of gallstones."

"It's well, the gallbladder is a little sack that holds fluid from liver and sometimes—mostly in very heavy people—it gets stones in it and sometimes the stones cause it to hurt."

"My dad is pretty fat, but where would he get a bag of stones?" I asked him. This is a phony story, I thought. I never heard such a phony story. "My dad has a lot of gas," I said.

I guess he could tell I didn't believe him. "The stones form in the bag," he went on, leaning forward, serious, like I *had* to believe him. "It hurt so much, Kim, they took his gallbladder out."

"Took it out?"

"Operated. They were at he hospital all night before last when you called. She was even going to drive up for you, but she didn't want to leave him, and besides, the hospital doesn't allow ten-year-olds to visit." He sighed. "I stopped by last night to talk to you about it and kind of prepare you for today like your mom asked me to. But I thought, later, that the skunk attack was enough excitement for one night."

"Wait a minute," I said, "what does all this have to do with a divorce?"

He looked up, startled. Miss Planet was heading down the path toward us. "Nobody knows I called." he said. "Listen, it was probably the wrong thing for me to do. Certainly it was against the rules."

"Divorce?" I asked again.

He shook his head. "Your mother thought that was a crazy idea. She said she guessed you really were homesick."

"But it wasn't crazy. Everybody . . . " I could feel my face turn red as I realized what it was. It was Telephone. It was Camp Trotter—Damp Daughter. It was Mrs. Fox's voice shouting across the gym and the ladies at the booth where I bought chances. Lewis hadn't known anything after all. ". . . a lot of pain," he was saying, "but your mom said he's smiling again. It'll be OK. She said to tell you."

Miss Planet reached us, her whole face a question. "Can I help?" she asked.

My stomach was churning. Mr. Ivanovitch looked at me and I shook my head at him.

"No, it was just . . . " he said.

"I had a . . ." we both started talking at once. Miss Planet waited, but neither of us went on.

"There might not be any scrambled eggs left if we stay out here much longer," she said.

I ran ahead, wondering how much he'd tell her. For two nights and almost three days I'd worried about phony things. And now I was so glad my parents weren't divorced I wasn't even scared about real stones in a sack. The woollyworms were gone.

After cold scrambled eggs, we packed our bags and stripped our beds. Mr. Ivanovitch gathered us around for our last outdoor Education project. The Scotch Tape was scheduled for orienteering. That meant we were supposed to find our way with compasses. Only we didn't stick together. After Mr. Ivanovitch talked about poles and paces for a while, he split us up into twos. Michelle and I were a team. He gave us paper with stuff written on it like "Go NNE 5 paces. Go 59 paces," so that at the end you'd expect to dig for Bluebeard's treasure chest and giants' bones.

My pace wasn't the same as Michelle's, but at last we found our gold treasure anyway, hanging from a tree branch—two bananas in a brown bag.

Wolfing them down, we made our way back to the clearing that was the meeting place for our group. Sam and Lewis were there playing catch with Mr. Ivanovitch's hiking boot. They hadn't gotten a list of SSW and NE 13 paces stuff like we had.

Instead, their paper had told them to find the boot, and fast. And they had. But they were tossing it so high, it was going to end up as a bird nest if they weren't careful.

Mr. Ivanovitch was off orienteering with Vinny because they were an uneven number of kids in my group. I hoped their path wasn't covered with thorns or broken beer-bottles, because those yellow-and-white stripes weren't going to keep out much.

"Look what I found," Sam called tossing the shoe at Lewis with one hand and holding up a piece of paper with the other.

"It's a rubbing. We found it in a bush, like it was growing there," Lewis said, grabbing the pitch. "There must have been a cyclone last night to drag it so far from the graveyard."

"I didn't hear a wind," Sam said.

"There was a lot of action," I told them, "after midnight."

"And I suppose *you* were out after midnight?" Sam laughed.

"Can I see the paper?" I asked him, knowing what it was.

"*I* found it," Sam said, holding it behind him.

"But it's mine," I told him.

"Prove it."

"It's a purple cupid with a moustache."

He turned around, peeked inside the rolled-up paper, and then looked back at me, very suspicious.

"How did you know?"

I shrugged. "I know because it's mine."

"But it rained the night we were at the graveyard, and this rubbing hasn't been rained on. A car's run over it, though." He flipped it past me so I could see the track on one corner.

"If you'd asked me about the tracks, I could have told you about them, too," I lied. I almost snatched it, but Nicky would have killed me if I'd torn that one too.

Lewis leaned over and fingered the tyre tracks on the paper. "You sure don't take good care of your stuff to have it, like floating around under cars."

"OK," Sam demanded, "explain about why it didn't get wet."

"You wouldn't believe me."

"You're right."

Mr. Ivanovitch came jogging up with Vinny, a bag of banana peels in his hand. ". . . climbed sheer cliffs when I was on Outward Bound," he was telling her. And then he saw the rubbing of the angel.

"Oh, Sam, you have my picture! Wherever did you find it?" He held out his hand.

Sam put the rubbing behind his back again and stepped away. "Kim said it was hers. She described it. Can you?"

Mr. Ivanovitch looked flustered. "But it's . . ."

Nicky and Arthur ran up behind Sam and Lewis, the fourth pair back.

"Sam," Nicky yelled, spotting the angel. "I take back everything gross I ever said about you. You've found my rubbing. I thought it was gone for good."

"Your rubbing?" He held it out at arm's length and stared. "What's so incredibly cueshee about this, anyway? Mine was much better. This angel has a moustache."

"Oh, does it?" Mr. Ivanovitch cried. "That's fantastic." Suddenly he raised his chin up high, held out both hands, and said, "Sam Fox, I'd like two things, and I'd like them promptly. First, I'll take my shoe, and," he smiled at Nicky and me, "and then I'll have *my* rubbing."

Sam blinked, looked at us to see if we'd complain and, when we didn't, handed them over. Then he turned away and, shrugging like he wouldn't care less, pulled Lewis on the ground with him. They started balancing acorn caps on twigs.

Mr. Ivanovitch handed us the rubbing. "Sign it in small letters-both-of-you-down by the tyre track," he said, taking a red pen from his big pouch and handing it over. "Not that I'm likely to forget. It's just that I'm framing it to hang in a special place, so it ought to be signed."

I could imagine our rubbing right over a fireplace with candles burning on each side. And I could see him and Miss Planet standing in front, smiling up at it.

"You gonna put your boot on now?" Nicky asked him.

"Maybe not," he told her, tilting his head. "I'm just getting used to walking askew."

"What I want to know," Sam said, "is *when* you guys did that rubbing, whichever of you did it." He flung an acorn top, like a frog's Frisbee. "I've been thinking, and I don't know when it could have been. There just wasn't any time."

"Some things are mysteries that will never be solved, Sam," Mr. Ivanovitch told him, and he hurried off to greet two more banana eaters.

For lunch I was hopper again for hot dogs and potato chips. Then we played one last kickball game up on the high field, the smell of skunk still faint in the air. The story was, Miss Planet told us, that a farmer's dog had tangled with a skunk and lost. I was glad we hadn't barked kitty-kitty.

The score was four all when Emily shouted. "The buses, they're here!" She didn't had her eyes off the road for the whole game. The buses were off the road for the whole game. The buses were pure sunshine. I had never noticed before that they smile. These were grinning from fender to fender.

After I tossed my little red suitcase up to the driver, who was parking them in the bus, I looked back one last time at Camp Damp Daughter lodge. Somebody had hung his underwear on the sign.

I settled down on a window seat. The heater was on, so it felt steamy, like August.

"What's that smell?" Nicky asked, holding her nose and looking at me. I smelled it, too. It was near. People were staring. Nicky broke up and dug a rose perfume-drenched Kleenex from my pocket and tossed it toward the back of the bus. It smelled like predator-prey. And it smelled like Mrs. Fox, too.

"Better than skunk," she said, laughing. I poked her in the ribs, but it isn't at all bad, the smell of roses. As the bus moved, my head felt heavy and my eyes kept flapping shut. Whenever I thought of the gallstones I remember Mr. Ivanovitch saying, "It'll be OK," and the gallstones would disappear and turn to granite or marble or skipping stones across the lake I slept.

The bus was rumbling up Central Street toward school when I woke. Nicky was shaking my shoulder.

"Except for the green slime mountain," Nicky said, "and the wrecked semi that spilled three hundred porcupines on the highway, and Emily getting sick again in the back of the bus, you didn't miss a thing." I opened my eyes as wide as I could. She shook me again. "And if you don't wake up they leave you on and you go back for three more days of peanut butter and jelly stew."

"Three days!" I shook my head. It seemed a whole lot more like three weeks we'd been gone.

"We played Animal, Vegetable, and Mineral while you were zonked out," Sam said, turning around in his seat.

"Yeah," Nicky moaned. "We played it a lot. One time you were the answer. You were vegetable."

"Nicky!" Lewis yelped. "That's not true, I *never* called Kim a vegetable."

"Maybe not," Nicky said, shrugging, "but you laughed when we said 'animal'."

I rubbed my eyes and focused on the group waiting on the side walk, peering at the buses. Mrs. Ezry was there, aiming her camera, waiting for the After shot. My mother was at work. Or at the hospital. Mrs. Ryder was going to pick Nicky and me up, but she wasn't around either.

Mr. Nagel and Mrs. Fox were already waiting on the steps of the school. Either our buses were slow or Mrs. Fox had been hot-dogging it down the highway in her Honda trying to beat us back.

As we climbed off the bus, Mrs. Fox stepped forward and boomed, "Welcome home. Welcome home after your wonderful adventure." And when Mr. Ivanovitch stepped off, she said, "Boys and girls, there's going to be an announcement. I'm sure there is Mr. Ivanovitch—has something to tell you all." She beamed.

Mr. Ivanovitch stuck his hands in his pockets. "I'm not sure. What if something . . ." Miss Planet grinned at him.

"Go ahead , Jack. Tell them. They'll be tickled," she said.

Sam tightened his lips and crossed his arms to keep the news out.

Behind us two mountains of bags were rising on the side-walk where the drivers were tossing them. Some kids were rushing off to get theirs, in a hurry to get home. Most of the 4B stood, though, with our mouths open, waiting, when a green van pulled up in front of the buses and a red-haired woman in a black-and-white check jacket bounded out. She hurried over to where we were standing like she was late, and I wondered whose mother she was. I'd never seen her before. As she walked she smiled at the ground instead of us, but when she looked up, it was straight at Mr. Ivanovitch.

He grabbed her hand and pulled her forward.

"I'd like you to meet my friends," he told her. She was only a couple of inches shorter than he was, but small. She was small and looked like she did not eat too much chocolate chip cheese-cake like my dad.

"This is Mr. Nagel, the principal, Mrs. Fox; Joan Planet; and these," he said, nodding at the group of us stacked up near the door of the bus, "these are a fraction of the 4Bs." She shook hands with us all. "This is Edwina Kinsella" he told us, like that explained everything.

When Edwina Kinsella finished shaking everybody's hands, she took his. And she held it. We stared, just as we had at his hand and Miss Planet's in the campfire circle.

"Is she your sister?" Arthur asked. Miss Kinsella grinned.

Mr. Ivanovitch took his hand away and reached for his green duffle just tossed on the stack.

"Are you a teacher?" Marshall asked Edwina Kinsella.

"Animal, vegetable or mineral?" I asked her.

She laughed. "I'm a telephone line-woman when the phones stop, I set them right."

"I was looking for her to say goodbye to us when we left for the camp," Mr. Ivanovitch told us, lugging the duffle bag to the group.

"An emergency," she apologized to him. "Some cable-TV guys sheared one of our lines. And a lot of wires were down night before last. Did it storm up by you?"

"Oh, yes," we said.

"Oh, wow."

"Lightning in the dark with sparks and ghosts."

"And a tree down by the lake."

"Oh, yes," we said.

"Is that," I asked him, "who you tried to call?"

"Right," he laughed. "She wasn't home either."

We followed along as he tossed his duffle into the back of the van. I hoped the landing didn't smash the angel.

Sam stepped forward and said, "What's this big announcement about you and Miss Planet?"

Mr. Ivanovitch threw back his head and laughed. "Sam, my dear, I think you were the only boy in 4B who wasn't trying to play matchmaker with me and Miss Planet."

Sam frowned. That was no answer.

"But," Lewis asked, "but which one are you going to marry?"

Mr. Ivanovitch eyed us all and shook his head. "Ah," he said, "while I do hate to disappoint you, I don't have plans to marry anybody."

I think Miss Planet smiled. She must have been worried, too.

Sam looked suspicious.

"Something you should know," Miss Planet said to us, filling in the silence, "is that fourth grade and fifth are going to be in the same hall next year. We're moving things around this summer."

"And I'm going to hang one of your gravestone rubbings in the new hall," Mr. Ivanovitch said, nodding to Nicky and me.

"You're hanging it?" Sam asked. "Why you?"

"Me," Mr. Ivanovitch answered, "because Mr. Nagel has asked me to come to central school next year to teach fifth grade." He looked around proudly. "Miss Swanduck is moving to Iceland. I'll be taking her place in 5B."

"Smile!" Mrs. Ezry called, kneeling down in the grass and aiming up at us. We smiled automatically, even Sam, while the programs in our head got rewritten.

"You," Emily said slowly, "are going to teach fifth grade at our school next year?"

"Yes," he told her, "my very first year as a regular teacher."

"That's really wonderful," she told him, and she shook his hand before heading off to where her mother stood waiting. She'd been waving to her and calling something in a language I didn't understand.

"Then," I said, suddenly realizing it, "we might get you next year."

"There are two teachers, so it's a fifty-fifty chance." He hopped into the van, rolled down the window, and called, "keep clear of crocodiles and creatures of the night." He waved at us with both hands as they drove away.

"Isn't that lovely," Mrs. Bosco said. She tugged at her cowboy kerchief. "Don't you think it's absolutely lovely, Sam?"

"I don't believe it. I don't believe Mr. Nagel would do that to us," Sam said, dragging his suitcase behind him.

"It's terrific," Arthur yelled, and ran to claim his bag.

"Smile," Mrs. Ezry called again, and those of us who were still left smiled.

"Kimberly," Mr. Nagel said, drawing me aside, "about our lunch at the Chuckwagon tomorrow."

"Oh, lunch," I told him, "I meant to tell you about lunch . . ." I'd totally forgotten to make up a foolproof excuse short of pneumonia. I wiggled my tooth with my tongue, but it hung in there. Too bad. It would have bled like crazy.

"Come to my office directly after the lunch bell . . ."

"No bidding, that's all right. I can just eat at school. They're having tuna casserole in the cafeteria tomorrow anyway, and that's my favourite."

Ruby stepped right up to see me suffer. She was swinging her sack of Articles to be left at Home, and she had a smirk as wide as a smiley face. When Mr. Nagel glanced at her, she was grinning so big, he smiled back.

"I have an idea," he said. "Why don't you bring one of your friends along . . ."

"But I . . ."

"Perhaps Ruby would like to join us." He looked at her with interest.

"Sure, Ruby," I said, whomping her on the back. "Mr. Nagel and I would like you to have a hamburger with us at the Chuckwagon tomorrow. Got any plans for noon? No, of course you don't. Noon is lunchtime. That's great."

"I . . . I . . ." she gagged.

"She'd love to," I told him. "She's just naturally shy. Thanks, Mr. Nagel."

As he hurried off to the office, I told her,

"It'll be a ball. Ruby, no kidding. We'll tell him all about trucking. And the next time you're in the office for skateboarding in the cafeteria, you'll have something to talk about."

Brong, brong. We jumped at the horn. Mrs. Ryder and Goby pulled up in their little gray station wagon. "Sorry to be late," she called as she climbed out, but I hurried over. "How is Dad?" I asked

"You already know?" She sighed. "Oh, good. I'd been worrying about how to explain gallstones. The dictionary didn't help." She leaned over till she was exactly my height and said, "Kim, he spent much too long pretending it didn't hurt, but he's OK. The doctor tells him he has to lose some weight, and your mother says "she'll hate that." She hurried over to hug Nicky. She hugged her back like she'd missed her too.

Goby, his dinosaur cape on wrong side out, bounced, *kapong*, out of the car. "Ribbit-roogie," she said.

"Hi, Gobe, who are you?" I asked him.

"Ribbit-roogie," he croaked again, springing forward on his toes.

"He's a frogosaurus," his mother laughed, "and he's been very jumpy waiting for you guys to come home."

"Did you put the fish to bed? Were these tarantulas?" Goby asked Nicky as she hurried to the car.

"Was there a lion?"

"There was a cat who thought he was an owl and there was a skunk called kitty-kitty," Nicky told him, and Goby laughed. He knew a good lie when he heard one.

"What did you do?" Goby asked me, grabbing me by the leg and digging his heels into the ground.

What I did, I thought, was make it through two nights with nobody but Mr. Ivanovitch and the woollyworms knowing how bad I wanted to be home.